A Jurassic Adventure

Dinosaur Cove™

Escape from the
Fierce Predator
and other Jurassic Adventures

by
REX STONE

illustrated by
MIKE SPOOR

Series created by
Working Partners Ltd

OXFORD
UNIVERSITY PRESS

Great Clarendon Street, Oxford OX2 6DP
Oxford University Press is a department of the University of Oxford.
It furthers the University's objective of excellence in research, scholarship,
and education by publishing worldwide in

Oxford   New York

Auckland   Cape Town   Dar es Salaam   Hong Kong   Karachi
Kuala Lumpur   Madrid   Melbourne   Mexico City   Nairobi
New Delhi   Shanghai   Taipei   Toronto

With offices in

Argentina   Austria   Brazil   Chile   Czech Republic   France   Greece
Guatemala   Hungary   Italy   Japan   Poland   Portugal   Singapore
South Korea   Switzerland   Thailand   Turkey   Ukraine   Vietnam

Oxford is a registered trade mark of Oxford University Press
in the UK and in certain other countries

British Library Cataloguing in Publication Data

Data available

ISBN: 978-0-19-273790-8

1 3 5 7 9 10 8 6 4 2

Printed in Italy
Paper used in the production of this book is a natural,
recyclable product made from wood grown in sustainable forests
The manufacturing process conforms to the environmental
regulations of the country of origin

CONTENTS

1. Escape from the Fierce Predator 9

2. Finding the Deceptive Dinosaur 99

3. Assault of the Friendly Fiends 191

FACT FILE

➡️ JAMIE AND HIS BEST FRIEND TOM HAVE DISCOVERED A SECRET CAVE WITH FOSSILIZED DINOSAUR FOOTPRINTS AND, WHEN THEY PLACE THEIR FEET OVER EACH OF THE FOSSILS IN TURN, THEY ARE MAGICALLY TRANSPORTED TO A WORLD WITH **REAL, LIVE DINOSAURS!** EXPLORING THE JURASSIC WORLD WITH THEIR DINOSAUR FRIEND WANNA IS AWESOME. BUT YOU NEVER KNOW WHAT COULD BE LURKING AROUND THE NEXT CORNER...

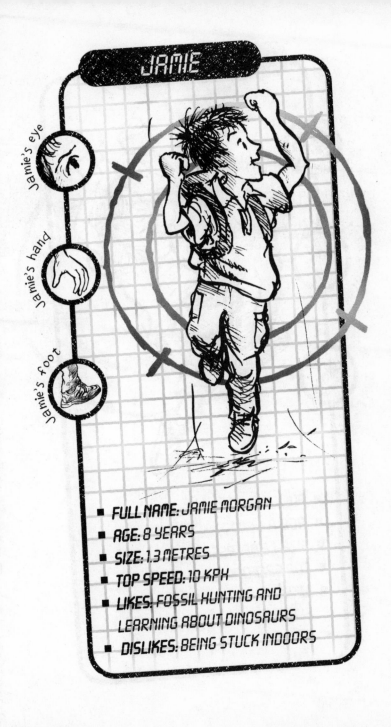

JAMIE

- **FULL NAME:** JAMIE MORGAN
- **AGE:** 8 YEARS
- **SIZE:** 1.3 METRES
- **TOP SPEED:** 10 KPH
- **LIKES:** FOSSIL HUNTING AND LEARNING ABOUT DINOSAURS
- **DISLIKES:** BEING STUCK INDOORS

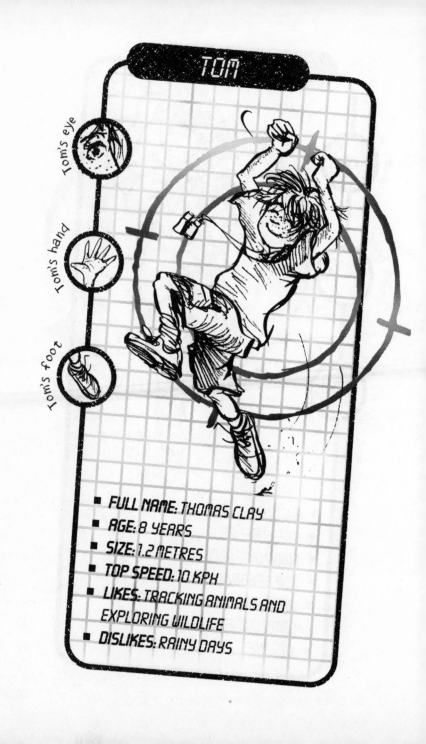

TOM

- Tom's eye
- Tom's hand
- Tom's foot

- **FULL NAME:** THOMAS CLAY
- **AGE:** 8 YEARS
- **SIZE:** 1.2 METRES
- **TOP SPEED:** 10 KPH
- **LIKES:** TRACKING ANIMALS AND EXPLORING WILDLIFE
- **DISLIKES:** RAINY DAYS

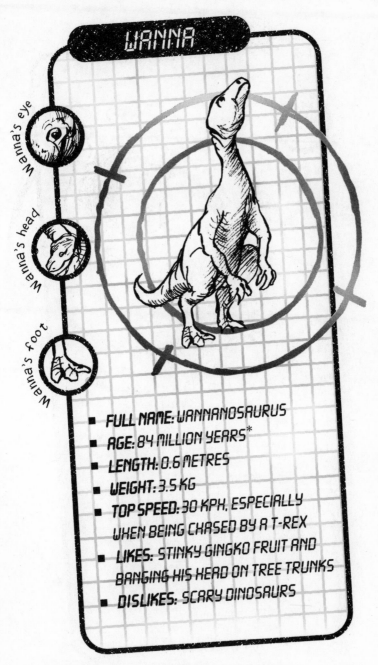

WANNA

Wanna's eye

Wanna's head

Wanna's foot

- **FULL NAME:** WANNANOSAURUS
- **AGE:** 84 MILLION YEARS*
- **LENGTH:** 0.6 METRES
- **WEIGHT:** 3.5 KG
- **TOP SPEED:** 30 KPH, ESPECIALLY WHEN BEING CHASED BY A T-REX
- **LIKES:** STINKY GINGKO FRUIT AND BANGING HIS HEAD ON TREE TRUNKS
- **DISLIKES:** SCARY DINOSAURS

*NOTE: SCIENTISTS CALL THIS PERIOD THE LATE CRETACEOUS

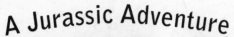

A Jurassic Adventure
Dinosaur Cove™
Escape from the Fierce Predator

Special thanks to Jan Burchett and Sara Vogler

For Claire Heywood, Nick Teare and Kevin Dawson
from Auntie Sara! – R.S.

These illustrations are for Daniel and Thomas Ogles, and all
the children at St.Katherine's CE Primary School – M.S.

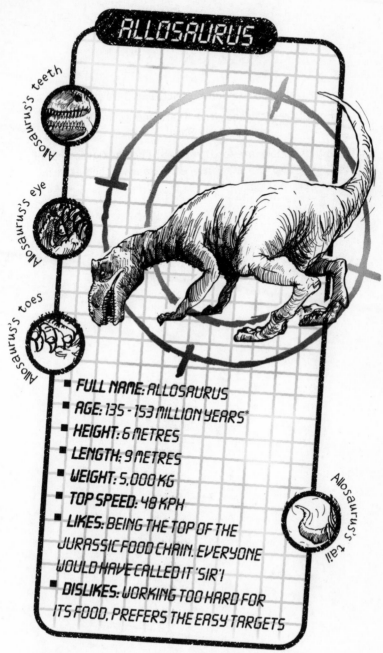

ALLOSAURUS

Allosaurus's teeth

Allosaurus's eye

Allosaurus's toes

Allosaurus's tail

- **FULL NAME:** ALLOSAURUS
- **AGE:** 135 - 153 MILLION YEARS*
- **HEIGHT:** 6 METRES
- **LENGTH:** 9 METRES
- **WEIGHT:** 5,000 KG
- **TOP SPEED:** 48 KPH
- **LIKES:** BEING THE TOP OF THE JURASSIC FOOD CHAIN. EVERYONE WOULD HAVE CALLED IT 'SIR'!
- **DISLIKES:** WORKING TOO HARD FOR ITS FOOD, PREFERS THE EASY TARGETS

*__NOTE:__ SCIENTISTS CALL THIS PERIOD THE JURASSIC

CHAPTER 1

SEARCH:

ABCDEFGHIJKLMN
OPQRSTUVWXYZ
1234567890 !?.,

'Quiet please, everybody,' Jamie Morgan called, waving his arms to get the attention of his dino-mad audience.

Jamie's best friend Tom Clay cleared his throat and used his best

TV presenter voice. 'The great
dinosaur quiz is about to begin.'

Jamie's dad handed out the last
clipboard and pencil to the crowd
of eager children and gave Jamie and
Tom high fives. 'Thanks for your help,
guys,' he said. 'I can take it from here.'

'I wish we could join in,' whispered
Tom as they stepped away.

'It wouldn't be fair,' Jamie
reminded him. 'Dad said we're such
dino experts we'd be bound to win.'

Tom nudged Jamie. 'He has no
idea!'

The boys had discovered an
entrance to a secret world of living

dinosaurs. It was hidden deep in the cliff, inside an old smugglers' cave, and they visited it as often as they could.

Jamie's dad read the first question, taken from a talk he'd given earlier that day. 'Which dinosaur was one of the biggest Jurassic predators and had a name that means "different lizard"?'

There was a noisy tapping of pencils as everyone wrote the answer down.

'Easy,' murmured Jamie.
'Allosaurus.'

After a couple more easy questions, Jamie's dad said, 'Now you'll have to put on your thinking caps. What newly discovered dinosaur from the Cretaceous period had slender arms and long bones in the hand with claws that look like sickles? It was probably covered in feathers.'

'That's hard!' whispered Jamie, trying to remember. 'I think it's a therizinosaurid.'

Tom nodded in agreement. It didn't look as though many people were writing down an answer. 'Newly discovered dinosaurs are tricky.'

Jamie's eyes lit up. 'I've just had an idea! What if *we* discovered a dinosaur that *no one* knew about?'

'And I know just where we could do that . . . ' said Tom.

Jamie knew what Tom was thinking. 'Dino World here we come!'

Jamie grabbed his backpack and waved to his dad. The boys sprinted

out of the lighthouse towards their
secret world.

'Off on another adventure?'
Jamie's grandad called as the boys
passed him fishing on the beach.

'You bet!' Jamie replied.

Soon the boys were in their secret
cave and Jamie flashed his torch over
the fossilized footprints on the floor.

'Here we go!' he said, placing his
feet in the footprints. Tom
followed close
behind.

In an instant they were in the hot Jurassic sunshine of their amazing secret world.

Grunk!

A little green and brown dinosaur bounded up.

'We're back, Wanna,' cried Jamie as their prehistoric friend gave them a nudge with his hard, bony head.

The wannanosaurus wagged his tail in excitement.

Tom looked around the cycads and conifers of the steamy jungle.

'Where would be
the best place to find
an undiscovered dino?'

'Let's climb that tree and look
around,' suggested Jamie.

The conifer branches were
well spaced and the fern-like
leaves easily pushed out of
the way. Tom and
Jamie climbed the
tree like a ladder.

Grunk?

A puzzled Wanna watched
them from far below as the
boys scaled the tree

almost to the very top.

'Awesome!' said Tom, looking through his binoculars. He turned an excited face to Jamie. 'You won't believe what I've just seen.'

Tom handed Jamie his binoculars and Jamie followed Tom's directions.

'Allosaurs!' Jamie gasped. 'A whole herd.'

Out on the open plains, he spotted a group of fierce-looking dinosaurs with big heads and long, thick tails.

'It's not an undiscovered dinosaur,' Tom said. 'But *we've* never seen one before.'

Jamie kept watch through the binoculars. 'Are they asleep? They're not moving much.'

'A rare find, indeed,' said Tom in his wildlife presenter voice, peering into an imaginary camera. 'Not just one allosaurus—the king of the Jurassic beasts—but . . . ' He squinted and tried to count. 'Twenty of the elusive dinosaurs. What could these ferocious creatures be up to?'

'There's only one way to find out,'
Jamie piped up. 'We've got to get
a closer look.'

The boys climbed down the tree to an excited Wanna. Tom collected several gingko fruits from nearby and stuffed them into Jamie's backpack. 'In case we need to keep Wanna quiet.'

They hurried through the thick
undergrowth, heading westwards for
the plains and the allosaurs. At the
edge of the jungle, Tom pointed to
a small outcrop of rocks about the
length of a swimming pool from
the herd and not too far from the
treeline.

'We can hide behind those
rocks and observe,'

said Tom. 'But watch for any signs
of allosaur movement.'

The boys crept over the dry plains
with Wanna at their heels and
crouched behind a large rock. Wanna
hunkered down next to them.

'What a great view!' whispered Jamie. He peered round the rock and studied the sleeping allosaurs. The beasts surrounded a huge dinosaur carcass. 'Dinner time's over, I reckon.'

'Now they're having a nap,' Tom added, pretending to snap a photo with an imaginary camera.
The allosaurs were hunched down, squatting on their powerful back legs. Their heads were bent forward on their chests. Dino bones, nearly picked clean, were scattered among the sleeping beasts.

Jamie pulled out his Fossil Finder and typed in '*ALLOSAURUS*'.

'THE LARGEST CARNIVORE OF THE JURASSIC PERIOD, UP TO TWELVE METRES IN LENGTH,' he read. 'LONG CLAWS ON THREE-FINGERED HANDS, AND LARGE, POWERFUL JAWS. HUNTED IN PACKS AND HAD A GOOD SENSE OF SMELL.' Jamie looked up at the carnivores. 'Uh oh. What if they smell us?'

'The wind is coming from the north,' said Tom, holding a wet finger in the air. 'Unless the wind changes, they won't be able to smell us.'

A pterosaur screeched
overhead and disturbed
two of the smaller
allosaurs who woke up and
began to nudge each other playfully.

'The adults are taking a well-earned
rest after a successful hunt,' said Tom
into an imaginary microphone. 'The
youngsters have other ideas. Their
bellies may be full, but they're not
going to waste time snoozing.'

One of the young allosaurs
knocked the other into an adult
allosaurus, waking it up. The largest

allosaurus got to its
feet and gave a roar.

'Nap's over,' Jamie
said nervously, hoping
the wind wasn't going to
change. He didn't
want any of those
allosaurs to come
looking for a tasty
boy-sized pudding.

Most of the group
woke up, shook
their heads, and

stamped their feet, crushing the remains of their dinner. Jamie held his breath.

The allosaurs began moving across the plains away from the rocky outcrop, and Jamie exhaled. Soon, all the allosaurs had stalked off, except for one still dozing in the sun.

Wanna began to fidget.

'Sorry, boy,' said Jamie. 'We're not ready to go just yet. There's still one allie that's not leaving.'

'It's still asleep,' Tom said. 'See its front legs twitching. Like a dog when it dreams.'

Wanna stood up and began to

33

nudge the boys.

'Wanna thinks it's
playtime,' Jamie said, scratching
Wanna under his chin. 'Why don't
you give him a few gingkoes to keep
him quiet?'

Tom rummaged in Jamie's

backpack for a gingko. As soon as
Tom held up the round, ripe gingko,
Wanna lunged for it, knocking it out
of Tom's hand. Tom and Jamie
watched in horror as the gingko

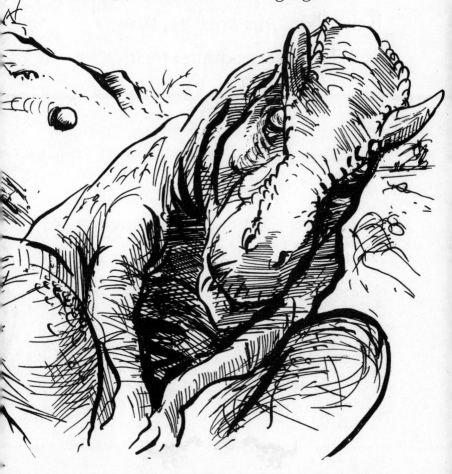

rolled across the ground, stopping just in front of the sleeping allie.

Before the boys could stop him, Wanna darted after his favourite snack right up to the allosaurus. If the allosaurus woke up, Wanna would be its after-dinner treat!

The boys whispered furiously at Wanna to come back, but the little dino was too focused on searching for his snack.

Tom waved another gingko at him but they couldn't get Wanna's attention.

'We've got to go and get him,' Jamie said.

Tom groaned and the boys crept out from behind the rock, closer and closer, until they could almost touch the bulky body of the sleeping beast. Its mouth was slightly open and they could just see the long, sharp teeth.

'Listen to it snore!' whispered Jamie.

'Look at those claws,' said Tom. 'They're as long as my hand.'

Just then, the allosaurus snorted in its sleep, making the boys jump.

'Let's get Wanna and get out of here,' Jamie decided.

The boys grabbed Wanna, who had just found the gingko, and pulled him to the safety of a clump of ferns nearer to the jungle.

'That's as close as I ever want to get to an allosaurus,' Tom said.

'It was pretty amazing,' Jamie said, glancing back to make sure the allie was still asleep.

Each boy grabbed one of Wanna's front paws and began to walk towards the thick jungle.

The air was suddenly full of
a hideous stink.

'Phwoa!' Tom gasped. 'What's
that horrible smell? It's worse than
a gingko fruit.'

'Wasn't me.' Jamie laughed, and
then spotted several brown,
steaming mounds nearly as tall
as he was just ahead.
'Allosaurus poo!'

'Gross.' Tom grinned.
'You'd need a huge pooper-
scooper for that lot.'

'And a million cans of air
freshener!' Jamie chuckled. 'Why
didn't we smell this before?'

'The wind must have changed,'
Tom said. He paused, realizing what
he had just said.

'If we can smell the poo, then that means that . . .' Jamie started.

'The allie can smell us,' Tom finished.

The boys and Wanna turned round just in time to see the huge, sleepy allosaurus open one eye.

The allosaurus lifted its head and sniffed the air.

'Uh oh,'  whispered Tom. The boys and Wanna backed away quickly.

The great beast moved its head slowly from side to side. 'It's trying to work out the strange new smell,' said Jamie. 'It won't be long before it decides we're pudding.'

'Let's get to the trees!' Tom shouted.

The allosaurus raised itself off its haunches and slowly lumbered in their direction.

The boys shot off across the plains with Wanna galloping at their side.

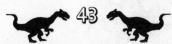

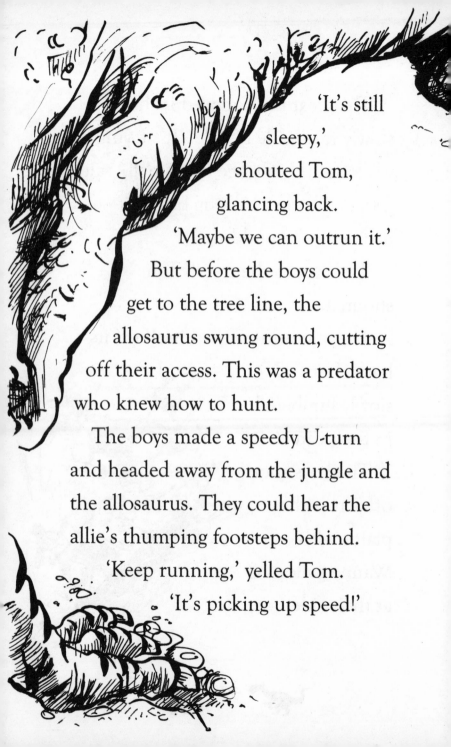

'It's still sleepy,' shouted Tom, glancing back. 'Maybe we can outrun it.' But before the boys could get to the tree line, the allosaurus swung round, cutting off their access. This was a predator who knew how to hunt.

The boys made a speedy U-turn and headed away from the jungle and the allosaurus. They could hear the allie's thumping footsteps behind.

'Keep running,' yelled Tom. 'It's picking up speed!'

The boys and Wanna raced forward through the now rocky terrain. The ground began to steadily slope upwards. It was hard to sprint—and the allosaurus was getting closer.

Suddenly, Jamie skidded to a halt. 'Oh no!' he groaned, looking down at the huge, deep canyon below him. One wrong step and they would tumble over the edge. There was nowhere left to run.

'It's the massive canyon,' said Tom in a panic. 'What are we going to do?'

Jamie turned to see the allosaurus bearing down on them. 'We're dead meat.'

'Look!' Tom shouted. 'There's a ledge down there.'

Jamie saw the shelf of rock beneath them. It was just wide enough . . .

'We've got to jump!' yelled Tom.

Grabbing Wanna, the boys took
a deep breath and jumped onto
the narrow ledge. All three landed
safely and looked up to the edge
of the canyon.

A terrifying roar sounded over their heads and

SNAP!

Sharp teeth gnashed in the air just above them. The boys and Wanna flattened themselves on the ledge. They could feel the allie's hot breath on the back of their necks.

The allie roared in fury

and stamped its feet, sending down
a shower of rocks and dust.
It couldn't lean over far enough
to reach them.

'It's having a tantrum because
its pudding has escaped.' Tom gave
a wobbly grin.

With each pounding step above
them, more earth and stones from
the walls of the canyon rained
down on them.

CRACK!

A fissure appeared in the rock
they were lying on.

'What if the ledge breaks from all
that stomping?' hissed Tom.

'Then we're in even bigger
trouble,' Jamie replied.

Wanna cowered against the
tumbling rocks and backed along
the ledge, grunking in terror.

Another loud crack sounded—the
ledge was splitting away from the wall!

When Jamie looked back, Wanna
had disappeared.

Tom and Jamie crawled along the
cracking ledge to where they last saw
Wanna and heard a distinct grunk.

Jamie looked towards the
wall and saw an opening with
a pair of beady eyes staring at him.

Grunk! Grunk!

Wanna had found a small cave
in the wall of the canyon. The boys
squeezed in after him, away from
the treacherous ledge. 'Well done,
Wanna,' he said. 'You've found us
a really good hiding place.'

Wanna grunked happily.

'Once the allie gets bored we can escape,' said Tom as they listened to the angry stamping overhead.

But the sounds of bellowing grew louder. Wanna cowered behind Jamie.

'Don't worry, Wanna,' said Jamie. 'We're safe here.'

'I'm not so sure,' said Tom, and pointed to the mouth of the cave.

Shards of rock showered down from the cave entrance as the allie's massive feet pounded above.

'It's going to collapse!' Tom shouted.

The boys and Wanna leaped back just in time.

54

CRASH!

The rock above the cave mouth tumbled down, sending up clouds of dust. The cave was plunged into darkness.

'I can't see a thing,' whispered Tom. Jamie felt round in his backpack for his torch and pulled it out. A huge pile of stones and rocks was blocking their exit. 'We're trapped,' he said.

'We'd need a bulldozer to shift that lot,' said Tom. 'What do we do now? We're stuck in a cave, millions of years in the past.'

Jamie shone his torch over the cave. The jagged walls stretched away into the dark. 'Maybe there's a way out this way.' Jamie took a tentative step forward.

'Let's see where it goes,' Tom said.

Bent double, Jamie led the way over the sloping, slippery floor. Jamie soon had to take off his backpack to squeeze through the narrow passage. The air became cooler as they went deeper underground.

At last the tunnel opened up and
they could walk along without
stooping.

'Look at these
scratches!'
Jamie shone his
torch on the
wall. 'And
there's more on
the floor, too.'

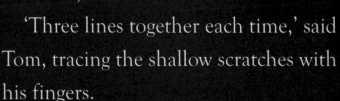

'Three lines together each time,' said
Tom, tracing the shallow scratches with
his fingers.

'They could be claw marks,' said
Jamie. 'A dinosaur must have come
this way.'

'One with big feet,' agreed Tom. 'Those marks are deep.'

'That's great news.' Jamie walked faster.

'Coming face-to-face with a vicious, sharp-clawed dinosaur isn't great news,' Tom said.

'It means there might be another way out of here,' said Jamie. 'The dinosaur that made these marks couldn't have squeezed through the narrow tunnel behind us. It came in from somewhere else.'

'Good thinking!' exclaimed Tom.

Wanna grunked, ran ahead and turned, his head cocked.

Jamie laughed. 'I think he wants us to hurry up!'

The boys moved along the tunnel faster now, until it split into two passages.

'Which one do we take?' Tom wondered.

Jamie examined the two tunnels in the torchlight. 'The scratch marks go

along the one on the right. If we follow them we might find the way out.'

Jamie walked down the tunnel, but Tom didn't move. 'Did you hear something?' he whispered.

Jamie shook his head. Just as he took a step forward, a short, high-pitched screech filled the air. Jamie stumbled back into Tom.

'There is definitely something

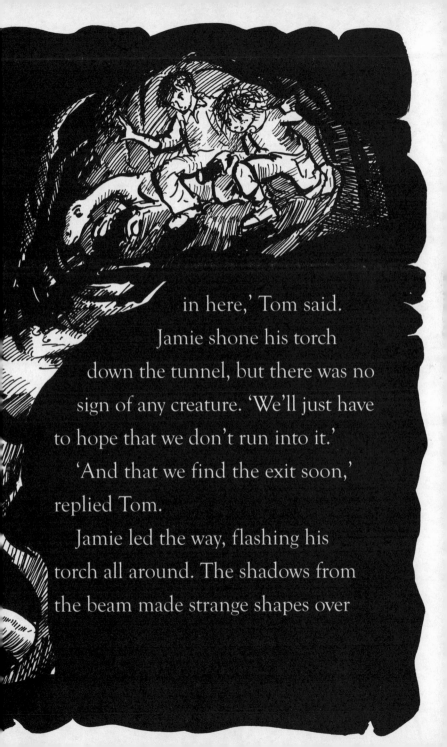

in here,' Tom said.

Jamie shone his torch
down the tunnel, but there was no
sign of any creature. 'We'll just have
to hope that we don't run into it.'

'And that we find the exit soon,'
replied Tom.

Jamie led the way, flashing his
torch all around. The shadows from
the beam made strange shapes over

the craggy walls. Tom followed with Wanna, keeping as close as he could to the light.

Suddenly, something darted across the beam of the torch ahead.

'What was that?' whispered Jamie in alarm, trying to catch the creature in the light.

'I don't know!' Tom said. 'But it's heading this way!'

SCREEE!

A dinosaur burst out of the darkness towards them. Wanna gave a frightened grunk.

But Jamie stood his ground. 'If it's used to the dark it won't like this.'

He held up his torch and shone it into the dinosaur's eyes.

As the bright beam flashed down the tunnel, the boys caught a glimpse of two monstrous yellow eyes glaring at them.

The creature gave a sharp cry and cowered back into the shadows.

'It's working!' exclaimed Tom.

But the words were hardly out of his mouth when another ear-splitting screech filled the air and the dinosaur was upon them, rearing up to attack. Long, sharp claws reached towards Jamie. He flung his arms up to protect himself and the torch fell from his hand.

Terrified, the boys cowered back into the darkness of the tunnel; Wanna pressed close between them. They could hear the torch being banged against the cave walls and the tunnel was filled with strange flashes of light.

'It's smashing my torch!' cried Jamie.

There was a CRACK! and the tunnel was plunged into complete darkness.

'We're in big trouble,' Jamie said, trying to feel his way back along the tunnel. 'It knows its way in the dark— and we don't.'

'I think it's coming!' Tom whispered.

The boys frantically hurried down the tunnel, scraping their arms and legs. Wanna was grunking with fear.

'We're where the tunnel divides,' came Tom's voice. 'Let's go down this other one.'

'And let's hurry!' Jamie replied.

'Suppose the dino *lives* underground,' panted Tom as they stumbled blindly along. 'There might not be another way out.'

'There has to be,' said Jamie.

The new tunnel twisted and turned, and they could feel the

ground sloping upwards as they scrambled to escape the dinosaur. It was catching them up and the boys could hear the hiss of its breathing.

'There's light ahead!' exclaimed Jamie.

They could dimly see the tunnel opening out into a cavern. They ran towards it.

Through a small crack in the high roof was—daylight!

'Our escape route!' cried Tom, pointing to a steep path up to the opening.

SCREEE!

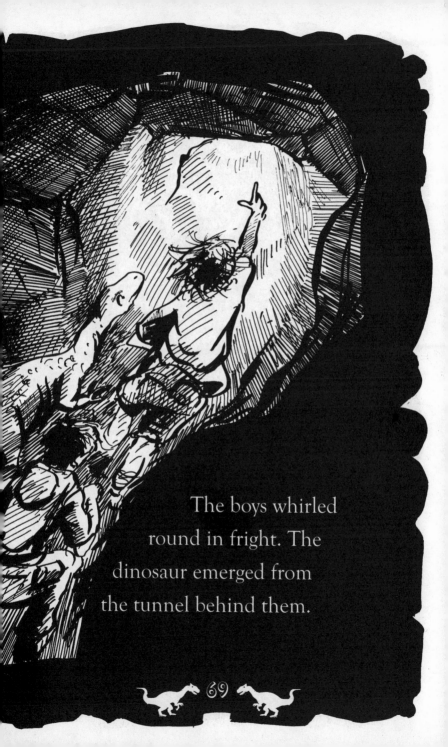

The boys whirled
round in fright. The
dinosaur emerged from
the tunnel behind them.

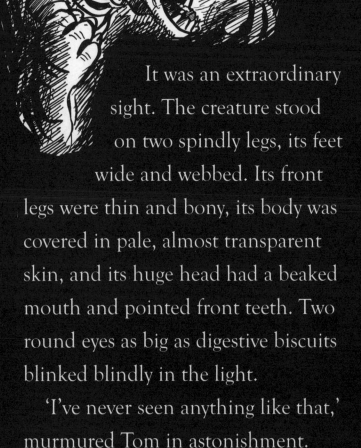

It was an extraordinary sight. The creature stood on two spindly legs, its feet wide and webbed. Its front legs were thin and bony, its body was covered in pale, almost transparent skin, and its huge head had a beaked mouth and pointed front teeth. Two round eyes as big as digestive biscuits blinked blindly in the light.

'I've never seen anything like that,' murmured Tom in astonishment.

'Whatever it is, it's still got my torch!' exclaimed Jamie. The strange dinosaur was brandishing the broken torch in its long claws.

As its eyes got used to the light, it moved towards the boys and Wanna. The three friends inched back, never taking their eyes off it.

Jamie reached into his backpack and pulled out a gingko. 'I'll try and hold it off while you see how we get out.'

Jamie threw the
fruit at the
dinosaur while
Tom dashed
across the cavern.
The gingko hit it
square in the chest
and it leaped back
with another shriek. Jamie
threw a second one.

Grunk!

Wanna didn't like watching his
gingkoes sail away.

The mysterious dinosaur dashed
towards Jamie again just as he threw
another fruit. The gingko landed

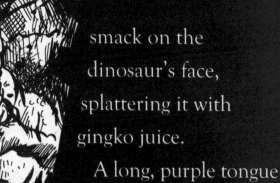

smack on the dinosaur's face, splattering it with gingko juice.

A long, purple tongue licked the juice off its face, and the dinosaur stopped charging. Then it dropped the torch on the floor, took a squashed gingko in its claw, and began to eat it with great slurping noises.

From across the cavern and partway up the steep path, Tom called out, 'There are footholds. We can make it!'

Jamie watched the pale, skinny dinosaur eating the gingko. It didn't look very aggressive any more, gobbling up the gingko fruits. Jamie took another gingko, just in case, and crept towards the big-eyed dinosaur.

'What are you doing?' Tom hissed.

'Trying to get the torch back,' Jamie said slowly and calmly. 'We can't leave anything in Dino World, remember?'

He took one step, then another.
He could almost reach the torch.
Jamie rolled the gingko fruit to the
dinosaur's feet and, while it grabbed
the fruit, Jamie snatched the torch.

EEE EEE EEE!

The dinosaur was enjoying the
gingkoes and didn't make a move
when Jamie backed away towards
Tom and the path up to the top of

the cavern. It looked as if their scary dinosaur was vegetarian after all.

'Let's get out of here,' Tom said, tempting Wanna up the steep climb to the hole in the cavern roof using a gingko. He held it out to make Wanna stretch as high as he could to bite it, and Jamie pushed Wanna from behind.

Grunk!

Wanna scrambled up the steep wall of the cavern, with his favourite food just out of reach. Jamie clambered up after him and at last they were near the opening. They could see blue sky above.

'We're almost out,' Tom said.

But when Jamie looked closely he could see that the hole was much too small, even for Wanna. 'We'll never fit through.'

'We have to,' Tom said. 'There's no other way out.'

Grunk!

Wanna took two steps back, charged forward, and, with a tremendous thump, headbutted the rock.

'It's cracking,' said Jamie. 'Wanna to the rescue!'

The little dino rammed the opening
again. Stones and earth fell away.
Then he squeezed through and
disappeared.

'Hooray!' the boys cheered.

Jamie and Tom pulled themselves
through the hole. At last they

were lying on their backs in the hot sunlight, with Wanna galloping round in delight.

'Clever boy.' Jamie patted Wanna on the head. 'You deserve a gingko feast.'

'Hey, we're back where we started,' said Tom. 'At the top of Massive Canyon.'

Jamie got out his Fossil Finder. 'Let's find out what that weird dino was.' He started tapping in its details.

'Lives underground,' said Tom. 'Eats fruit, and has huge eyes!'

Jamie studied the screen. 'I can't find anything,' he said at last. 'I've put in all the details . . . but there's no match.'

Tom gasped. 'Do you think that means . . .'

'We've found a new dinosaur!' Jamie shouted.

ROOAAR!

The boys swung round. The
allosaurus was still peering over
the edge of the canyon.

'Oh no!' exclaimed Jamie. 'It's still waiting for a Tom and Jamie pudding.'

'Maybe if we creep across the plains,' whispered Tom, 'it might not spot us.'

They hurried across towards the jungle as quickly and quietly as they could.

Jamie looked back to see the allosaurus sniffing around where they had come out of the cavern. Then it turned to face them.

'I just hope the wind doesn't change,' Jamie said.

ROOAAR!

The allosaurus waved its head

angrily and began to stomp towards them, sniffing every few steps.

'We need to mask our scent,' said Jamie. 'Then we won't smell so tasty.'

'Got an idea,' yelled Tom, veering off in another direction. 'But you're not going to like it.'

'I'll like anything

better than being allosaurus pudding,' Jamie shouted back.

'Then follow me!' Tom sprinted faster. Wanna ran alongside.

As the allosaurus charged across the plains towards them, Jamie suddenly realized where Tom was heading—the piles of steaming allosaurus poo.

'Oh no!' he yelped.

'It's our only chance,' insisted Tom.

ROOAAAAR!

Jamie didn't need telling twice. Keeping his mouth and eyes tightly

closed, he dived into the stinking
mess.

PLUMPH!

Tom and Wanna joined him.
Jamie could feel the ground
shaking with the approach of the
allosaur, and then things went still.
Jamie forced his head out of the
sticky poo and opened his eyes. The
allie was towering over them. Tom
and Wanna popped up beside
him. 'Keep still,' he muttered,
trying not to open his
mouth.

The allosaur
looked about and
sniffed the air
uncertainly.

It stamped its feet a few times. At last it lumbered off.

'Phwar!' Jamie and Tom burst out of the brown pile and shook like a couple of wet dogs, sending flecks of allie poo flying everywhere.

Wanna was covered as well, but he didn't seem to notice the dreadful smell.

'There's only one place I want to be now,' said Tom. 'In the shower!'

'Agreed,' nodded Jamie. They set off across the plains and into the thick jungle, washing themselves as much as they could at the first stream they came to.

When they reached Wanna's
cave they picked him a huge
pile of gingkoes and left
the little dinosaur
munching happily.
They stepped
backwards in the
dino prints back into
Dinosaur Cove, and the moment
they were in the smugglers' cave what
was left of the allosaurus poo turned
to dust.

Tom laughed. 'I wish the smell
would go too.'

Jamie went to pull out his torch
but then remembered, 'That cave

dino broke my torch. We'll have to feel our way out.'

Once out of the cave, the boys rushed back to the lighthouse and escaped into the museum office to avoid the crowd of visitors.

'While we're here, let's research our mystery dino,' Tom said, scanning the rows of dino books.

'I'll try the Build-a-Dino program,' Jamie said. He sat down at his dad's computer and typed away.

WOW!

'Beak, claws, cave dweller . . . '
After entering the colour,
the size of the eyes, and the
noise it made, he hit the enter
key.

'That's close enough,' said
Tom as an image appeared
on the screen. 'Is there
a match?'

Jamie held his
breath, and then the
words 'UNKNOWN
DINOSAUR' flashed
across the screen.

'Wow!' said Tom.
'We really

UNKNOWN
DINOSAUR

discovered a dinosaur.'

The boys did a high five.

'Hello, boys.' Jamie's dad came
in with an armful of posters and
glanced at the screen. 'That's one
weird dinosaur you've invented.'
He put the posters down on a shelf.
Then he sniffed the air. 'Phwar!
Can you smell something? It's like
rotten eggs!'

Jamie grinned at Tom.

'What are you going to call your
new dinosaur?' Jamie's dad asked.

'Hmm,' Tom replied. 'Maybe
caveosaurus . . . or screechiosaurus . . . '

'I've got it.' Jamie laughed.
'Torchbreakiosaurus!'

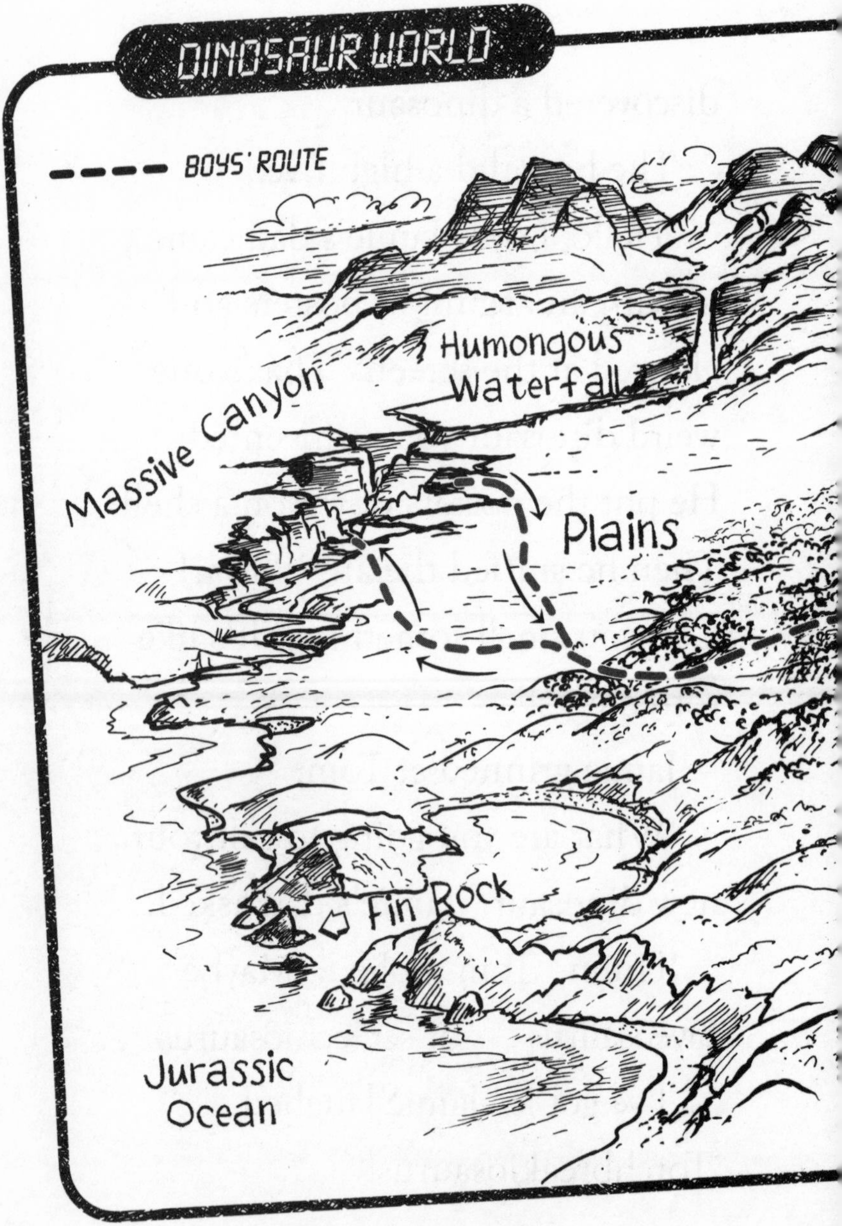

DINOSAUR WORLD

- - - - BOYS' ROUTE

Humongous
Waterfall

Massive Canyon

Plains

Fin Rock

Jurassic
Ocean

Misty
Mountains

Thick Jungle

Gingko
Cave

Discovery
Hills

A Jurassic Adventure

Dinosaur Cove™

Finding the
Deceptive Dinosaur

Special thanks to Jane Clarke
For Sara Grant, you rock like a fossil – R.S.

For Krista Clark and the children of The Hebron
Elementary School, Ohio, USA, who like Dinosaurs a lot
and long may you continue to enjoy! – M.S.

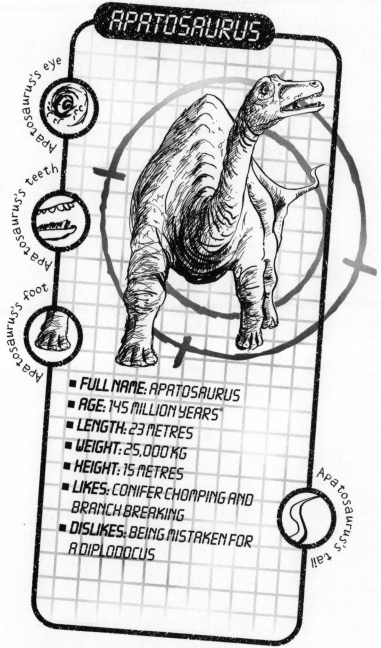

APATOSAURUS

Apatosaurus's eye

Apatosaurus's teeth

Apatosaurus's foot

Apatosaurus's tail

- **FULL NAME:** APATOSAURUS
- **AGE:** 145 MILLION YEARS*
- **LENGTH:** 23 METRES
- **WEIGHT:** 25,000 KG
- **HEIGHT:** 15 METRES
- **LIKES:** CONIFER CHOMPING AND BRANCH BREAKING
- **DISLIKES:** BEING MISTAKEN FOR A DIPLODOCUS

*NOTE: SCIENTISTS CALL THIS PERIOD THE JURASSIC

CHAPTER 1

'That is a serious pile of dino puke,'
said Jamie Morgan as he studied
a plate-sized stone with crusty grey
flakes and chunks sticking out. This
fossilized dinosaur vomit was the

centrepiece of a temporary exhibit in his dad's museum.

'That dino must have been *really* sick,' Jamie's best friend Tom Clay agreed, raising his voice to be heard against the rain battering the old lighthouse. 'I reckon it needed to see a vet!'

'Imagine being a dino doctor and a t-rex turned up with a sore throat,'

Jamie said with a grin. 'And you had to take its temperature.'

'Or if you had to give an allosaurus its shots,' Tom said.

'Or treat a triceratops with tricerapox,' Jamie added.

'Or a diplodocus with diarrhoea!'

'Sick!' Jamie and Tom fell around laughing as Jamie's dad walked over. 'Scientists don't think the dinosaur was ill,' he said with a smile. 'If you look hard, you can see the crusty bits are fossil belemnite shells.

It's ichthyosaur vomit—the sea creatures would eat the soft bits and regurgitate the hard parts.'

'Like owls spit up owl pellets after they've eaten a mouse?' Tom asked.

'Exactly. Fossil vomit is important new scientific evidence,' Jamie's dad said. 'It's very rare. We don't often get to see what dinosaurs were eating.'

Jamie grinned. Dad didn't know it, but he and Tom knew lots about dinosaur eating habits. They'd been on the menu themselves a couple of times in Dino World—the secret world they'd discovered full of real, live dinosaurs.

'The rain is slowing down,' Tom said. 'Time for some exploring?'

Jamie nodded. 'I'll get my backpack!'

'Don't forget coats and wellies,' Dad called after him.

Jamie reappeared with his backpack and an armful of bright yellow raincoats and green rubber boots.

'Got the ammonite to take us back to the Jurassic?' Tom whispered as they pulled them on.

'In my backpack.' Jamie slung it over his shoulders. The boys stepped out into the pouring rain, hurried across the beach, and squelched

along the cliff-top path to the
smugglers' cave.

'Dinos will spot us a mile off in
these raincoats.' Tom stripped off his
dripping wet yellow raincoat and
bundled it up behind a rock.

Jamie did the same. He couldn't
wait to be in Dino World again!
Quickly, he led the way through the
gap at the back of the cave into the
secret chamber that only they knew
about. With Tom close behind him,

he fitted his wellies into the first of a line of fossil dinosaur footprints that led across the floor of the cave.

'One, two, three,' Jamie counted the prints as he stepped towards what looked like a solid cave wall, 'four . . . FIVE!'

On the fifth step, the ground squished beneath his feet and he and Tom were back in Dino World.

A little dinosaur with a very bony
head was curled on a nest of leaves
beneath the overhang of Gingko
Cave.

'Wake up, Wanna,' Tom said,
giving Wanna's head a stroke.
'It's time for a new adventure.'

Wanna wagged his tail feebly, but didn't get up.

'That's strange,' Jamie said with a frown. 'Usually, he's all over us.'

'This will get him on his feet.' Tom plucked a stinky gingko fruit and held it under Wanna's nose. Wanna looked at the fruit and burped gently.

'Maybe he's ill,' Jamie said, worriedly. 'Wanna *always* gobbles up gingkoes.' He put his hand on the little dinosaur's scaly forehead. 'He's really cold and clammy.'

'That's because he's cold blooded and he's lying in the shade,' Tom said. He knelt down and put his ear

to Wanna's chest. 'His heart sounds
OK to me, and I can't hear any
rattling when he breathes.'

'Let me listen.' Jamie pressed his
ear against Wanna's scales. He could
hear a gentle hissing as the little
dinosaur breathed and the steady
thud-thud-thud of his heart.

Uuurp!

Wanna's burp was so sudden and so loud that Jamie jumped. Wanna got to his feet, too.

'I don't think there's much wrong with him,' Tom said, holding out the gingko. 'I'd burp if I ate these stinky things.'

Wanna turned away his head.

'He's probably eaten too many and upset his stomach,' Jamie agreed. 'Let's get going. The sunshine and exercise will do him good.'

He plunged into the steamy Jurassic jungle, through the dripping ferns and conifers, to the edge of the plains where they had seen dinosaurs

before. In front of them was a small group of enormous long-necked plant eaters grazing on the tops of the trees.

'What are they?' Jamie wondered.

'I'm not sure.' Tom stepped onto a rocky outcrop to get a better look. 'They're bigger and heavier than the diplodocus we met, and darker green.'

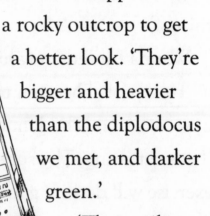

'Their tails aren't as long, either. I'll check.'

Jamie took the Fossil Finder out

of his backpack, typed in
'*JURASSIC PLANT EATERS*', and began to
scroll through the list. 'They're
apatosaurs,' he said. 'The name
means deceptive lizard.'

'Like a spy lizard?' Tom said.
'Cool!'

'The Fossil Finder says that
scientists thought they had discovered
a new dinosaur—the brontosaurus—
but it turned out to be an
apatosaurus all along,' Jamie
explained.

'This looks like an apatosaurus
family,' Tom said as Jamie stowed
the Fossil Finder in his backpack.

'That big one with the wrinkly skin looks like the grandad.'

'Then those two patties must be the mum and dad,' Jamie indicated the two largest apatosaurs.

'And their two kids,' Tom laughed, pointing to the younger dinosaurs rearing on their back legs and jostling their necks to get at the best branches.

'There's a really young one!' Jamie exclaimed. 'Under the old one's legs.'

As they watched, the old pattie broke off a branch from the tree and carefully lowered it to a pony-sized pattie with smooth light-green skin. The small one dropped the heavy branch.

Hoo-hoo! The little one started to squeak.

The old pattie stopped chewing and looked around. *Hooo!*

The other patties froze and took up the call. *Hoo! Hoo! Hoo!*

'What's upsetting them?' Tom was looking in every direction.

Beside them, Wanna began to quiver.

'I think he's afraid, too.' Tom looked at Jamie.

'And when Wanna's afraid,' Jamie said nervously, 'it means trouble is on the way.'

Two leopard-spotted two-legged dinosaurs burst out of the jungle and hurtled across the plains.

The patties stood frozen to the spot as the predators ran towards them, close enough for the boys to

make
out the
crimson horns on
the end of their noses
and their evil-looking teeth.

'Ceratosaurs!' Tom and Jamie said together.

Suddenly, the patties turned and scattered, fleeing closer to the stony outcrop where the boys were standing.

'Hide!' Tom yelled. The boys and Wanna dropped down into a gap between the rocks. They cautiously peeped out. The apatosaurus family had gathered back together at the edge of the rocks and turned to face the predators. The littlest one hid between the old pattie's legs, near the centre, while the other pattie kids disappeared behind the mum and dad.

The ceratosaurs slowed and stepped towards the patties menacingly.

'They're as big and scary as that allosaurus that chased us,' Jamie murmured.

The ceratosaurs tilted their big yellow heads to one side and looked first at the smallest pattie and then at each other. Drool started to dribble from their ferocious jaws, and then one trotted to the left of the patties, one to the right.

'They're hunting together,' Jamie whispered. 'They're going to attack from both sides.'

The patties were backing round to form a circle, their heads facing out. The old one nudged the youngest into the centre.

The ceratosaurs glanced at one another and, side by side, began to circle the ring of huge apatosaurs.

'The ceratosaurs are looking for a weak point,' Tom whispered. 'That little pattie's their target.'

'That's horrible.' Jamie shuddered.

'Predators have to eat.' Tom tried to sound matter-of-fact. 'It's no different from a lion targeting a young wildebeest. Young ones are just easier to catch.'

'I've seen that on TV,' Jamie agreed. 'Old and sick animals are easy targets, too.'

Suddenly, the ceratosaurs lunged at one of the patties. The pattie quickly turned and thrashed its tail at them. The predators leapt out of the way.

'That must be the pattie's only defence,' Tom guessed. 'The impact of that tail could break a predator's leg.'

The ceratosaurs took a few steps away from the patties.

'They're giving up.' Jamie breathed a sigh.

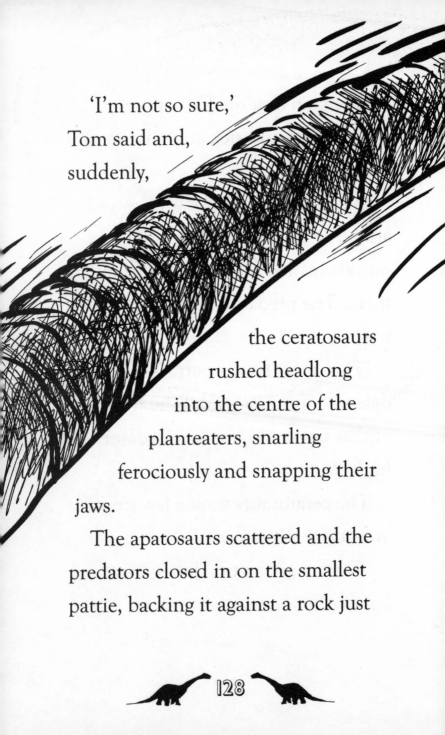

'I'm not so sure,' Tom said and, suddenly,

the ceratosaurs rushed headlong into the centre of the planteaters, snarling ferociously and snapping their jaws.

The apatosaurs scattered and the predators closed in on the smallest pattie, backing it against a rock just

in front of the
watching boys.
Hoo! Hoo! Hoo!
It squeaked
pitifully.

'We have
to do something!'
Jamie grabbed a rock.

But, before he could throw it, the old
pattie came charging back in between
the youngest pattie and the
ceratosaurs.

The ceratosaurs didn't hesitate

and changed course to attack the old
pattie. The old apatosaurus tried to
throw off the
ceratosaurs, but
their sharp teeth
sank deep into its
wrinkly flesh.

'Get off!' Jamie
screamed,
hurling his
rock. It bounced
off a ceratosaurus's
hard head. Wanna was grunking in
alarm.

'Take that!' Tom took careful aim
with a stone. It struck one of the

ceratosaurs in the eye
and it let go of its grip on
the old pattie's neck.

'And that!' Jamie's second
stone hit the horn of the second
ceratosaurus.

The ceratosaurs glanced up
towards the boys' hiding place, then
at each other.

'They've seen us!' Jamie ducked down into the rocks.

All around them, the ground began shuddering and quaking. Tom and Jamie peeped out.

'It's the rest of the pattie family,' Tom said, excitedly. 'They're coming to the rescue!'

The ceratosaurs took one look at the solid wall of dinosaurs charging towards them and fled across the plains. Jamie and Tom breathed a sigh of relief as they disappeared from view.

The old pattie fell to its knees as the rest of the family thundered up.

Its long neck and tail hit the ground with a thud. A pool of blood spread out on the earth beneath its neck and body.

'It's badly hurt,' Jamie said in dismay.

The apatosaurs gathered round the wounded dino, nudging it softly with their rubbery lips. The old pattie slowly lifted its head. Blood trickled down its neck as it gently nuzzled each of the family in turn. Then, one by one, the patties turned and shuffled away until only the youngest was left.

'I think they're saying goodbye,'

Tom said sadly, as he, Jamie, and Wanna clambered out of their rocky hiding place.

The youngest pattie lay down beside the old one and gently laid his smooth green neck over the old apatosaurus's wounds.

'We have to try and help!' Jamie said.

CHAPTER 3

Jamie, Tom, and Wanna scrambled down the rocks to the plains below. Wanna and the little pattie stood to one side as the boys examined the old apatosaurus. Rivulets of bright red blood were pouring from its wrinkly neck, and bloody teeth marks dotted its back.

'These wounds are really deep,' Jamie groaned, looking at the vicious tears in the old pattie's skin.

'At school, in first aid, they told us to tie a tourniquet around an arm or leg to stop it bleeding,' Tom told Jamie, 'but we can't tie something round its neck.'

'If only we could sew up the gashes . . .' Jamie sighed as a wheezing sound came from the old pattie's throat.

'Even if we could, I don't think that would fix it,' Tom said. 'It's not breathing well at all.'

The old pattie stirred.

'It's trying to get up. Perhaps it'll be OK,' Jamie said.

They backed away as the old pattie struggled to its feet. It towered higher than a house above them.

'At least it doesn't seem to be in too much pain,' Tom said. 'It isn't going crazy like that diplodocus with the toothache.'

The old pattie bent its head and gently nuzzled the young one. For a long moment they stood muzzle to

muzzle, then the old one gently pushed the young one away. The young one's head and tail drooped as it turned to follow the rest of its family.

The wounded pattie stomped slowly away in the opposite direction, leaving a trail of bloodspots.

'We have to keep the meat eaters away from it! Come on, Wanna,' Jamie coaxed. The little dinosaur's tail was drooping. 'You can't stay here; the ceratosaurs might come back.'

Wanna followed slowly as the wounded pattie plodded across the sun-drenched plains.

'It seems to know where it's going,'

Jamie said after they had come to the edge of the plains and started a slow incline.

The pattie was travelling towards what sounded like waves crashing on a distant shore. As they walked on, the sound of gushing water grew louder and louder. They came to a line of dense trees and followed the old pattie as it pushed its way through the undergrowth.

They emerged at the bottom of the biggest waterfall Jamie had ever seen. It was so high and so wide that the mist from the water was spun with rainbows.

'Awesome!' he gasped, feeling
the cool, refreshing mist soak
into his skin.

The injured dino bent to take
a sip from the crystal clear pool at
the base of the waterfall.

'We've got to call this place
Humongous Waterfall,' Tom
declared, wiping the spray out
of his face. 'What a great place for
a sick dino to get better! Take
a drink, Wanna!'

Wanna sipped at the

cool water and wagged his tail.

Jamie shivered. 'Wish I'd brought that raincoat. It's cold!'

'I think it's making Wanna feel bet—' Tom began, but before he could finish speaking the little dinosaur started bobbing his head up and down, making strange hiccuping burps.

'What's wrong with him?' Jamie hurried towards Wanna.

Urp, urp, urp! Wanna burped. A thin orangey liquid was dribbling from the corners of his mouth.

'What's that?' Tom said in alarm. 'Open wide, let us have a look...'

146

The boys peered into Wanna's mouth.

The dinosaur opened it wide.

URP!

A spurt of cold, chunky vomit showered the boys from head to toe.

CHAPTER 4

'Urgh!' Tom wiped a glob of
mustard-yellow slime out of his eyes.

Wanna hung his head.

'He's *really* sick,' Jamie said,
shaking his head to dislodge the
crusty brown lumps of vomit stuck in
his hair. 'He might have caught
a dinosaur flu. That can make them
throw up.'

'Wanna's a Cretaceous dino in the Jurassic,' Tom said worriedly. 'He doesn't know all the plants. He might have eaten something poisonous.'

They watched as Wanna took another sip of water, then he turned and opened his mouth.

'Watch out!' Tom yelled.

Jamie leapt aside as the arc of vomit splattered on the rocks and spattered on his wellies.

Wanna looked up at him with a pleased grunking noise and wagged his tail.

'At least it's made him feel a bit better,' Jamie said. 'Perhaps he's

150

puked out whatever made him feel
ill.'

'Before we clean up we should take
a close look at it,' Tom told him. 'It's
scientific evidence for what he's
eaten, like that fossil
ichthyosaur vomit.'

He picked up
a stick and poked
the puddle of
puke.

'What are these big crusty brown flakes?' he asked Jamie. 'They look like scales, but Wanna's a plant eater.'

Jamie examined the lumps. 'They're bits of bark,' he said. 'That could be what's making Wanna feel ill.'

'Maybe he has thrown up all the bad stuff,' Tom replied.

'All over us.' Jamie shuddered. 'I've got to get it off before I throw up, too!' He waded into the pool beneath the waterfall and began to wash down his arms. 'This water's cold!' he exclaimed, raising his voice against the rushing waterfall.

'Freezing!' Tom agreed, swooshing his palm across the water so it drenched Jamie.

'Oi!' Jamie gasped, splashing him back.

'Wanna needs a wash more than me!' Tom laughed.

The boys scooped the cold water onto themselves and the little

dinosaur and washed away the dribbles of puke.

'That's better.' Jamie's skin tingled and his cheeks glowed as they stepped out fresh and clean.

'I hope the old pattie's feeling better, too!' Tom said.

The boys glanced to the spot where they'd last seen the wounded apatosaurus drinking, but the old pattie was nowhere to be seen.

'Where's that deceptive old dino gone?' Jamie joked.

'It must have left some trace.' Tom dashed over to the place where they'd last seen the old dino.

'Footprints!' he yelled. Jamie dashed over to look.

The tyre-sized prints were a mixture of water and blood. Wanna trotted over and sniffed at them. His head and tail drooped.

The trail of bloody footprints led round the pool to the base of the waterfall.

'It doesn't make any sense.' Tom frowned. 'It's a dead end. There's no way an apatosaurus could climb these steep rocks, even a young fit one.' Tom edged closer to the thundering fall. 'There's just one set

of footprints going in,' he shouted
over the noise of the water. 'Where
can he have gone to?'

CHAPTER 5

SEARCH:

'Perhaps he walked backwards in his own set of footprints,' Jamie yelled, following close behind Tom. 'That would be *really* deceptive.'

Tom shook his head. 'He must have gone through the waterfall. It's hard to see anything in this mist and spray . . .' He thrust his fist into the crashing waterfall.

'Ow!' he exclaimed, as the rushing water pummelled his hand.

'It'll beat us back if we go slowly,' Jamie bellowed. 'We'll have to make a dash for it.'

Grunk, grunk, grunk!

Wanna was looking agitated.

'Don't worry, Wanna,' Jamie bawled. 'We won't leave you behind!'

The boys grabbed the little dinosaur's stumpy arms and charged into the thundering water. The water stung their skin

and felt like a huge hand pushing them down. And then the boys emerged, sputtering, in a cave behind the waterfall. The cave was bathed in a spooky blue light that flickered as it filtered through the water.

'A secret cavern!' Jamie's voice was muffled by the sound of the rushing water.

The cave floor was littered with piles of white bones silhouetted against the dark rock.

'There are skeletons everywhere.'

Tom tried to pick up a leg bone that was as tall as he was, and nearly dropped it again because it was so heavy. He lowered it gently to the damp floor.

Wanna was cowering behind Jamie.

'It's OK, Wanna; bones can't hurt us,' Jamie reassured the nervous little dinosaur. 'I've seen a lot of dino skeletons in museums,' he told Tom, 'but never so many in one place.'

'They're all plant eaters,' Tom muttered. 'None of the skulls have fangs.'

Wanna followed the boys closely as

they picked their way through the enormous skeletons, dodging beneath the arches of rib bones and stepping carefully over long backbones. Every skull they found belonged to the same sort of dinosaur.

'Are you thinking what I'm thinking?' Tom murmured.

'It's an apatosaurus graveyard,' Jamie whispered, 'and that means . . .'

At the back of the cavern, furthest away from the light, a mountainous shadow stirred. It was the old apatosaurus.

 165

Tom looked at Jamie. 'My grandma says old cats often slip away to find a quiet place to die . . .'

'That's what the old pattie's done. It knows its time is coming,' Jamie said with a catch in his voice. 'Can we do anything?'

'Only keep him company.' Tom tiptoed towards the collapsed dino.

'I can hardly bear to look.' Jamie reluctantly tiptoed after him, followed by Wanna.

The old apatosaurus's neck was stretched out along the cool floor of the cavern. The bleeding had slowed to a trickle. Its eyes were closed,

and there were long pauses between
its shallow breaths.

'At least it doesn't look as if it's
suffering,' Jamie murmured.

At the sound of Jamie's voice, the old pattie half-opened its tired eyes.

Wanna crept next to the mountainous apatosaurus. With a huge effort, the old dino lifted its head from the floor and nuzzled him gently. Wanna curled up beside the dying dino as its head sank back to the ground.

'It's like they know it's OK; that this is the way it's meant to be,' Jamie

said, dashing away the tears that
suddenly filled his eyes.

He and Tom sat in silence next
to the old pattie's head and
gently stroked its wrinkly
scales. The old pattie gave
a sigh. It closed its eyes

again, and its huge body seemed
to relax. Little by little, the old
apatosaurus's gentle breathing
slowed . . . and stopped.

'It's dead,' Tom said quietly.

'It was peaceful, not scary at all,'
Jamie whispered, awestruck. 'Just
very, very sad.'

'A dinosaur that big must have
been over a hundred years old,' Tom
murmured. 'Most dinos didn't get to
live that long.'

'And it died saving the little one,'
Jamie added.

Time seemed to stop as they sat in
silence in the flickering blue light.

170

After a while, Wanna got to his feet.
He bobbed his head and turned
towards the waterfall.

'Wanna's right.' Tom sniffed as he
stood up. 'We should let it rest in
peace.'

They stood for a moment, heads
bowed, by the old pattie's body.
Then they grabbed hold of Wanna
and leapt through the waterfall. But
instead of bursting out into
sunshine, they found themselves in
shadows. Jamie looked up in
amazement. They were beneath
a canopy of apatosaurs.

'The family came to say goodbye,'

Tom said in
wonder as they
walked through the
archway of
apatosaurus necks
and out into the
blazing sunshine.

Behind them, the patties raised their heads.

Hoo! Hoo! Hoo! The apatosaurs were calling to the skies.

CHAPTER 6

Tom, Jamie, and Wanna looked
back towards Humongous Waterfall.
For a moment, an enormous
rainbow hung across the curtain of
water, then broke up into countless
smaller arcs.

They watched the huge dinosaurs
begin to munch on the tall conifer
trees. One of the larger patties broke

off a branch and lowered it
to the small one.

'It learned that from the old one.'

Tom smiled a wobbly
smile as the little
pattie munched
contentedly.

'Life goes on.
They can't just hang
around feeling sad.'

'Nor can we,' Jamie said. 'It's

time we went back. Do you think the patties will remember the old one?'

'They've already remembered how it picked branches,' Tom said. 'And Wanna remembers us from visit to visit. Dinos must have memories.'

'Perhaps they're like elephants and never forget,' Jamie murmured.

They followed their trail back across the plains towards Gingko Cave.

'We can't leave Dino World until we're sure Wanna's going to be OK,' Tom said as they approached the cave

'Course not,' Jamie agreed. 'He's looking much better since he threw up. He must have eaten something bad for him.'

'Like this tree!' Tom stopped by a tall tree with narrow leaves growing near the entrance to the cave. 'Look at the bark, it's all scaly. It's the stuff that was in Wanna's vomit.'

'It's not a gingko, or any sort of conifer.' Jamie took out the Fossil Finder and typed in TREE WITH SCALES. 'It's called a scale tree,' he read. 'VERY

COMMON BEFORE THE DINOSAURS, BUT MOST DIED OUT BY THE JURASSIC. There wouldn't have been any around for Wanna in the Cretaceous.'

Tom looked closely at the tree trunk. A strip of bark was missing from the bottom. 'It's been nibbled on recently,' he said. 'It must have been Wanna!'

'He's got to understand he can't eat this again.' Jamie pulled a chunk of scaly bark off the tree and pretended to eat it.

'Bleeeeeeergh!!' he

yelled, clutching his throat and staggering around. 'Bleergh, uuurgh! Uuuuuuurp!'

He pretended to throw up.

Tom held out a piece of bark to Wanna.

Gak, gak, gak! Wanna backed away.

Jamie laughed. 'I think he's got the message.'

'I'll pick him some gingkoes,' Tom said.

'And I'll make his nest more comfortable.' Jamie gathered an armful of soft moss. It felt good to be able to do something to help their dinosaur friend.

Wanna settled down in his nest
and licked at one of the gingkoes on
the pile that Tom had laid beside
him.

'He's getting his appetite back.'
Tom grinned. 'He'll be fine next time
we see him.'

'Bye, Wanna,' Jamie said, stepping
back in the footprints. 'See you
soon.'

The soft ground turned to rock
beneath their feet and in an instant
they were back in the secret chamber
of the smugglers' cave once more.

Tom and Jamie squeezed through
the gap, grabbed their raincoats, and
raced out of the cave and through the
rain to the old lighthouse.

They dashed upstairs to the kitchen.

'Atishoo!' Jamie sneezed, shaking raindrops everywhere.

'Uh oh,' Tom said. 'What if you've caught a prehistoric cold?'

'I can't have. We can't bring anything back,' Jamie reminded him.

'Only memories,' Tom murmured.

'I thought I heard you coming back.' Grandad came into the kitchen and took a long look at the cold, wet boys.

'Anything wrong?' he asked.

Jamie glanced at Tom. 'We're just a bit sad that . . . that dinosaurs died out.'

'Well, my boy, that's part of the circle of life,' Grandad said. 'After all, if dinosaurs hadn't become extinct, we wouldn't be here today.' He threw them each a towel.

'Thanks, Grandad!' Jamie said, wrapping the towel around his shoulders.

Grandad rumpled Jamie's hair. 'I'm glad there are no big scary

dinosaurs still lurking around
Dinosaur Cove.'

The boys stopped towelling off to
glance at each other.

'A dinosaur would make an easy
meal out of an old man like me,'
Grandad continued.

'I'm not so sure,' Jamie said. 'I've
heard that the older dinosaurs were
sometimes the fiercest.'

'You're right. I do make a fierce
cup of hot cocoa.' Grandad grinned.
'Now, who wants some?'

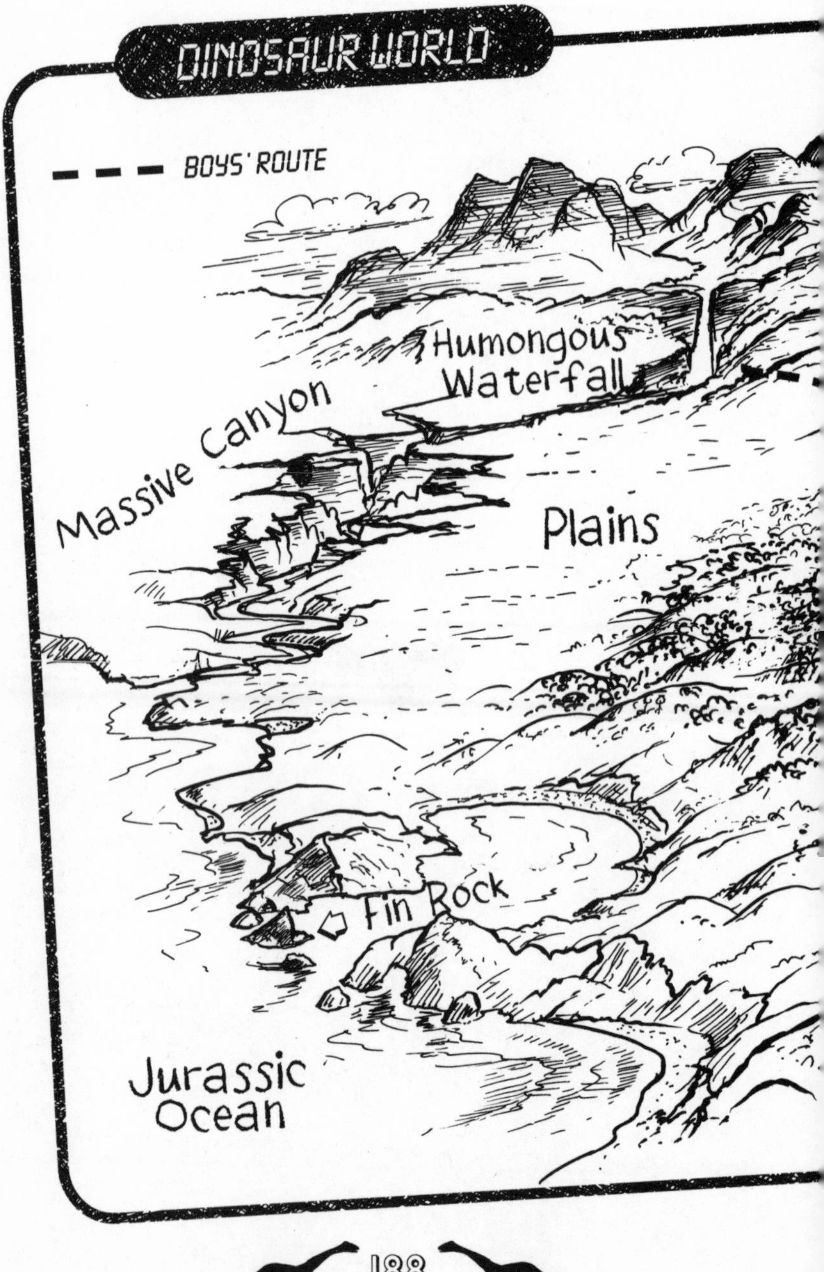

DINOSAUR WORLD

- - - BOYS' ROUTE

Humongous Waterfall

Massive Canyon

Plains

Fin Rock

Jurassic Ocean

Misty Mountains

Thick Jungle

Gingko Cave

Discovery Hills

A Jurassic Adventure

Dinosaur Cove™

Assault of the
Friendly Fiends

Special thanks to Jan Burchett and Sara Vogler

For Sara O'Connor and everyone at Working Partners — R.S.

These illustrations are dedicated to Sophie Butcher, Librarian, whose support for Dinosaur Cove is much appreciated — M.S.

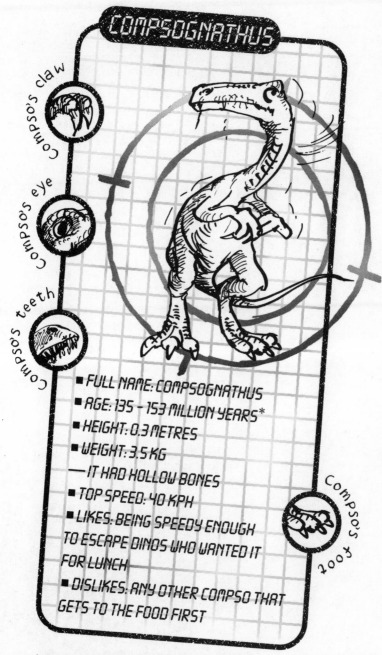

COMPSOGNATHUS

Compso's claw

Compso's eye

Compso's teeth

Compso's foot

- **FULL NAME:** COMPSOGNATHUS
- **AGE:** 135 – 153 MILLION YEARS*
- **HEIGHT:** 0.3 METRES
- **WEIGHT:** 3.5 KG
— IT HAD HOLLOW BONES
- **TOP SPEED:** 40 KPH
- **LIKES:** BEING SPEEDY ENOUGH TO ESCAPE DINOS WHO WANTED IT FOR LUNCH
- **DISLIKES:** ANY OTHER COMPSO THAT GETS TO THE FOOD FIRST

*NOTE: SCIENTISTS CALL THIS PERIOD THE JURASSIC

The dinosaur museum was alive with dinosaurs—tiny t-rex, a small pack of diplodocuses, grounded miniature pterodactyls, and a velociraptor arguing with a stegosaurus over who had the better costume. Jamie

Morgan and his best friend Tom Clay were herding them all into the activity room.

'I've never seen so many people here,' said Jamie.

Tom laughed as a little triceratops with lopsided horns raced by. 'Dress as a Dino Day was a great idea of your dad's.'

The two boys squeezed in at the back of the room as the children watched Jamie's

Pangaea
(before volcanoes
and earthquakes)

Pangaea
(after volcanoes
and earthquakes)

dad show film clips about the Jurassic
Age. Computer-generated stegosaurs
lumbered across the screen; then a
herd of allosaurs attacked a huge
diplodocus.

'Now,' said Dad. 'Let's look at the
landscape. It's just as exciting.' The
film showed a picture of a huge land
mass. 'This is Pangaea,' he told his

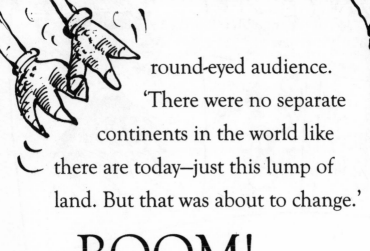

round-eyed audience. 'There were no separate continents in the world like there are today—just this lump of land. But that was about to change.'

BOOM!

An erupting volcano appeared on the screen. Shrieks of delight filled the room.

'The volcanoes and earthquakes broke up Pangaea like a jigsaw puzzle,' said Jamie's dad. 'That was the start of the continents we know now.'

'And now it's time for lunch!'
Jamie's dad announced. 'There are
sandwiches and crisps at the back, so
if you get in line . . . ' But the young
dinosaurs weren't listening. They
jumped out of their seats and surged
towards the food, chattering
excitedly.

'Here comes trouble!'
muttered Tom.

The boys leapt into
action. It was their job to
make sure every child had
a napkin, a plate, and
a sandwich. But a sea of

hands was trying to snatch the food
all at once.

'Slow down,' Jamie shouted above
the din.

'ROARRR,' answered an
ankylosaurus who was leaping in the
air to grab an extra packet of crisps
from the box in Tom's hand.

'Dinosaurs fight to get their food,'
growled a stegosaurus, pushing to the
front.

'That's not always true,' said Jamie,
giving Tom a wink.

The children stopped and stared at
him.

'Real dinosaurs, like ankylosaurs,

make a nice straight line and march one behind the other,' Jamie told them solemnly. 'I should know. I live in the dinosaur museum.'

The dinosaurs immediately shuffled into a line, arms—and wings—by their sides.

'That was brilliant!' Tom whispered to Jamie as he poured juice into dinosaur cups. 'I thought we were going to be trampled.'

Soon all the children had marched off, with some very realistic roaring, to eat their lunch.

Jamie stared at the image that was

still on the screen—the huge mountain ranges of the Jurassic era.

'No wonder the kids got excited,' he said, taking a handful of crisps. 'That presentation of Dad's was awesome.'

'Should we check out some real Jurassic mountains?' Tom whispered.

'Good idea,' Jamie agreed. 'We haven't explored the mountains in Dino World yet.'

The boys had a secret. Deep in the cliffs of Dinosaur Cove, they had found the entrance to a magical world of living dinosaurs. They went there whenever they could.

Jamie grinned. 'We've helped with lunch like we promised . . . '

At that moment Jamie's dad rushed past. 'Forgot to tell them to wash their hands before they hit the museum!'

'We're just going out for a bit,' Jamie told him.

'OK, see you later!' Dad was gone.

Jamie checked in his backpack. Everything was there: the Fossil Finder, notebook, and Jurassic ammonite to take them into the right dino time. He swung it onto his back.

Tom snatched up some ham

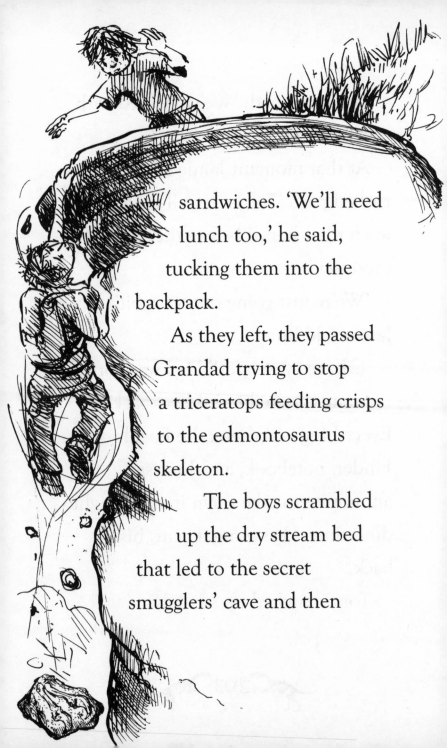

sandwiches. 'We'll need lunch too,' he said, tucking them into the backpack.

As they left, they passed Grandad trying to stop a triceratops feeding crisps to the edmontosaurus skeleton.

The boys scrambled up the dry stream bed that led to the secret smugglers' cave and then began to climb the boulders. Jamie reached for a handhold to pull himself over a ledge.

KERACK!

The rock split off in his hand and he lost his grip. Jamie was dangling by only one arm high above the ground!

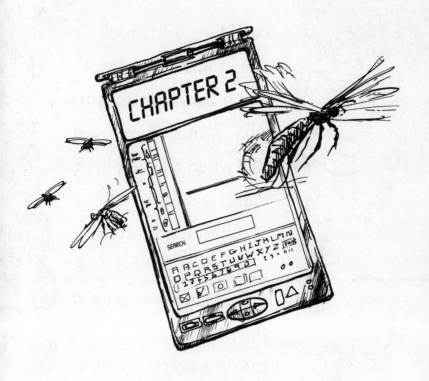

CHAPTER 2

SEARCH:

ABCDEFGHIJKLMN
OPQRSTUVWXYZ

Tom shot out a hand and grasped
Jamie's arm in a firm grip.

'Thanks!' breathed Jamie,
scrambling for safety as loose rock
and pebbles rattled away down the

boulders. 'One rock cracks and I nearly fall down the cliff. Imagine what it must have been like when the whole of Pangaea split apart!'

Climbing more carefully now, the boys pulled themselves up to the smugglers' cave and into the secret chamber.

'There are Wanna's footprints, waiting for us,' said Jamie, placing his trainers in the shallow dips on the stony floor. He felt the usual bubble of excitement as they followed the line of prints to the cave wall and . . .

A blast of hot air hit their faces and they found themselves stepping out of Gingko Cave amongst the giant trees of Jurassic Dino World.

'Phwah!' panted Tom, wiping his forehead. 'It's steamier than ever.'

'The trees are dripping with water,' said Jamie. 'Looks like we've just missed a rainstorm.'

Flickers of sunlight were breaking through the leaves of the huge trees above and drops of water plopped down on their heads. Suddenly the boys heard a rustling sound from the horsehair ferns in front of them. Spray flew up and soaked them as a dripping wet, green and brown dinosaur charged out of the undergrowth and skidded to a halt at their feet.

'Wanna!' exclaimed Jamie, wiping his face. 'Thanks for the shower.'

'Want to come mountaineering with us?' Tom asked, giving their dinosaur friend a scratch on his flat, bony head.

Grunk!

'I think that's a yes!' Jamie laughed as Wanna ran round in excited circles.

'The Misty Mountains are to the north.' Tom checked his compass. 'This way.'

They soon reached the edge of the stifling jungle. Ahead, the flat plains steamed in the heat and beyond rose the high peaks of the cone-like mountains, purple against the sky.

'They're awesome,' said Jamie.
'And look at those dark clouds above
them. I bet there's another storm
coming.'

'I think the dinosaurs have sensed
it,' agreed Tom, peering intently
through his binoculars. 'There's

hardly a sniff of life on the plains today.'

'What are we waiting for?' said Jamie. 'We don't want to get caught in the open by a prehistoric downpour.'

They set off at a sprint across the

plains, splashing through the puddles left by the rain. Wanna galloped ahead. At last they reached the green lower slopes of the Misty Mountains.

Jamie gazed up at the dark, rugged peaks towering above them, disappearing into the clouds. 'What a sight!' he breathed.

Grunk! The little dinosaur stopped and looked up as if puzzled.

'Yes, that's where we're heading, Wanna,' said Tom.

They started climbing through thick ferns, disturbing huge brightly-coloured insects as they went. But Wanna hung back.

'Come on, boy,' called
Jamie. 'It's just getting a bit
steep. You'll be OK.'

The little dinosaur
hesitated for a moment then
he trotted along behind them,
staying close to their heels. Soon
the vegetation stopped, and they
were clambering up the bare
rocks alongside a pebbly

stream. Wanna poked his head in and drank with huge slurping noises.

Jamie stopped and looked back to where the massive canyon ran across the plains down to the ocean. 'The water's heading for the canyon,' he said.

'Today history is being made,' announced Tom into an imaginary microphone. 'Our intrepid Jurassic trio are exploring the Misty Mountains. They are the only humans—and wannanosaurus—ever to attempt such a climb. Steam is rising from the mountainside as rainwater evaporates. What will they find? Does anything live in this strange place?"

EEK, EEK!

A shrill squawk filled the air. The boys froze.

CHAPTER 3

A beaky brown nose poked out
from the steaming ferns. Then a
whole head appeared, with little
bright eyes that swivelled this way
and that, checking the area. Finally a

strange creature, no bigger than a chicken, stalked out and shook itself. It took no notice of the two boys but scuttled away on stiff back legs towards the stream bed. Jamie and Tom snorted with laughter as its head darted down to drink and its tail bobbed up in the air.

Wanna cocked his head on one side. He looked puzzled.

'Have you ever seen anything so funny?' said Jamie, laughing.

'It walks like a cartoon dinosaur!' Tom spluttered. 'I've seen it in books but it's a lot funnier in real life.'

'It's a compsognathus,' said Jamie.

'But I don't know much about them.' He opened his Fossil Finder. '*PRONOUNCED KOMP-SOG-NA-THUS WHICH MEANS "PRETTY JAW".*'

'I wouldn't call that pretty!' Tom scoffed. 'What else does it say?'

'*SPEEDY TWO-LEGGED CARNIVORE,*' Jamie read on. '*ONE OF THE SMALLEST DINOSAURS.*'

Another beaky head popped out of the ferns. 'Looks like it's got a friend,' said Tom. Squawking, the newcomer scuttled over to the water.

'Wonder what they'll do if we go up to them.'

Tom began to climb over a rock to get to the drinking dinosaurs. But his foot slipped on some loose stones. 'Yaieee!' he yelped as he stumbled. Immediately the two heads shot up and two pairs of beady eyes studied Tom.

Yaieee! Yaieee! the creatures called back.

'Wow!' Jamie said as he hauled Tom to his feet. 'They're copying you.'

Tom made the noise again. This time four more heads appeared and

all the compsos joined in with the sound. Soon the calls of the mimicking creatures were bouncing off the rocks.

'You know how experts think some dinosaurs evolved into birds,' said

Tom. 'I reckon these compsos
became parrots!'

Grunting excitedly, Wanna darted
after a green and yellow striped
lizard, which scurried away from the
stream.

'That lizard has a purple head!'
exclaimed Tom. 'Never seen anything
like that before.'

EEK, EEK!

The compsos had
seen it too. They
scampered towards it in
a bunch, shrieking as the
lizard zigzagged over rocks
and under ferns, trying to escape.

'That lizard had better watch out,'
said Jamie, 'or he's going to be
compso lunch!' Wanna was left

behind as the eager little creatures
raced along after it.

'And the compsognathuses are
gaining on their prey,' announced
Tom into his pretend microphone.
'More have appeared. They're
fighting over it . . . can you hear
those angry chatterings? I think
it's going to get away . . .
No, the smallest

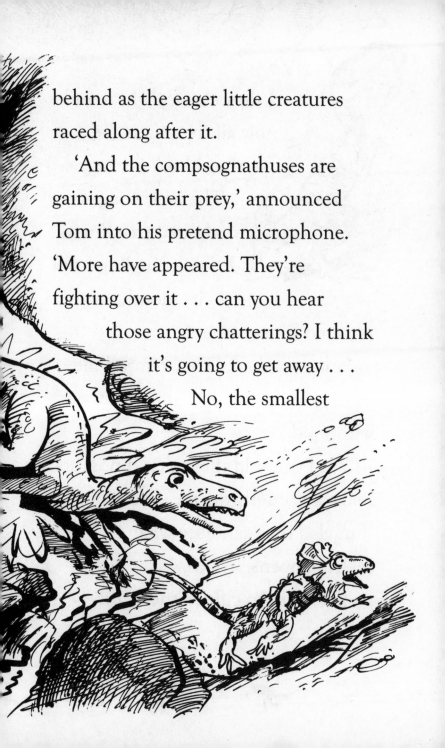

compso has caught it and
now all the others are
after him.'

The little compso
dashed past, lizard
tail dangling from
its mouth,
pursued by the others.

Jamie laughed. 'They remind me
of the kids at the museum—obsessed
with food.'

'And you told them that dinosaurs
make an orderly queue,' said Tom.
'I'm glad they can't see what
really happens.'

The compso gulped the lizard

down and the chase ended. The rest of the bunch began sniffing around, looking for more food. Then one strutted eagerly towards the boys.

'Look out,' said Jamie. 'We've got company.'

'It looks like a mini ostrich,' said Tom, as the little creature stalked round them, neck outstretched, sniffing their scent.

'It's very friendly,' said Jamie.

'And quite cute . . . Aah!' He leapt in alarm as the dinosaur suddenly jumped onto his back with a screech. 'Help!' he yelled. 'Its claws are digging right in.'

The determined compso started scratching at the top of Jamie's backpack.

'It's after the sandwiches,' called Tom. 'Oh no you don't, you little thief.' He grabbed the bird-like dinosaur round its waist and tugged. But it was surprisingly strong and clung on with its long claws. Jamie's arms flailed about as he tried to knock the creature off

and Wanna grunked anxiously around their feet.

At last Tom gave a great tug, pulling the backpack right off Jamie's back. The compso let go as the backpack crashed to the ground. Tom grabbed the pack as the determined dinosaur looked the boys up and down, searching for a way to get its snack.

Wanna grunked crossly at it, then waddled away up the steep mountainside.

'Good thinking, Wanna,' said Tom, putting the backpack onto his shoulders as Jamie rubbed at the

scratches the little creature had left on him. 'Let's go before any more get the idea that we're a tuck shop.'

'Agreed,' said Jamie grimly. 'Those compsos are not as cute as I thought.'

They set off after Wanna but soon found themselves surrounded by a crowd of chattering dinosaurs. Compsos darted out of the ferns and leapt at them from every rock and stone.

'Uh oh!' whispered Jamie. 'We're in big trouble now.'

CHAPTER 4

EEK,

EEK!

The little creatures jostled against the boys, pecking and scratching at their legs.

'We can't make a run for it,' said
Tom, looking around at the carpet of
chirping dinosaurs. 'There's nowhere
to put our feet.'

'They *are* just like the pesky kids at

the museum,' said Jamie. 'And that's given me an idea.' He reached into the backpack on Tom's shoulders, pulled out a sandwich, and waved it at the creatures. When he had their

attention, he tossed it into the ferns. The compsos were on it like a swarm of bees.

'Well done,' said Tom. 'Let's get away from here while they're busy fighting for it.'

'Too late,' groaned Jamie. 'They're coming back for more. Ouch!'

The hungry little compsognathuses were back, raking their sharp claws against the boys' knees.

'They don't mean any harm,' said Tom, trying to push them away, 'but they're hurting.'

Grunk, GRUNK!

Wanna was back, running around the crowd, trying to get to the boys.

'Yow!' Tom was suddenly pulled sideways. 'What's going on?'

'One of them has got the backpack strap,' called Jamie. 'They want more sandwiches.'

The hungry dinosaur gave a tug. Tom staggered as he tried to wrench the strap away. But now compsos from all around were joining in the tug of war and Tom was no match for them.

'Help!' he cried as he lost his balance and crashed to the

ground. Soon he was covered in chirping dinosaurs all searching for food.

Gerunk! Wanna came to his rescue. He butted and pushed the little creatures away. Jamie saw his chance. He grabbed Tom's arm and pulled him to his feet.

'Thanks . . . both of you . . . '
Tom was out of breath.

'How are we going to escape?'
Jamie wondered. 'They're
everywhere.'

'Let's try the ham decoy again,'
said Tom, taking Jamie's backpack off
and reaching into it. 'I'll try and
throw the sandwich a bit further this
time.' He lobbed it deep into the
nearby ferns.

Some of the compsos scampered off and started hunting for it.

'Run!' shouted Jamie, grabbing his backpack. 'While we've got the chance.'

But the other compsos weren't so easily fooled. They chased after the boys.

'Let's jump in the stream,' yelled Tom. 'Maybe they don't like getting wet.'

They splashed into the shallow water that trickled down from the mountain.

'It's working!' said Jamie, looking over his shoulder. 'They've stopped.'

The compsos were leaping about on the bank, squeaking and chattering crossly, but they didn't follow.

Tom, Jamie, and Wanna splashed upstream. Soon they had left the annoying little dinos behind. The banks were becoming higher as they climbed.

'Hey! Have you noticed something strange?' said Tom. 'The water's warm—really warm.'

'You're right,' agreed Jamie. 'Even though it's ice melted from the top of the mountain.' He peered up the stream bed. 'It's much steeper now.'

'And rockier.' Tom looked down at the jagged stones beneath their feet. 'See the way the rock has little holes in it? That means it's an igneous rock.'

'I remember Dad telling us about that,' agreed Jamie.

'Igneous rocks are made from magma.'

'And magma is the hot molten rock inside the Earth,' said Tom.

'Which only comes up when a volcano erupts,' added Jamie.

'And then it's called lava!' exclaimed Tom.

They looked at each other.

'That means . . . ' began Jamie.

'This Misty Mountain isn't just a mountain . . . ' said Tom.

'It's a dormant volcano,' finished Jamie. 'Awesome!'

'I'd love to have seen it erupt,' said Tom, his eyes shining. 'There would have been rumbling and shaking and rivers of lava streaming down.'

'Let's see if we can make it to the crater at the top,' said Jamie.

They scrambled over boulders, trainers slipping on the wet ground. Wanna kept close behind.

'Phwah!' gasped Jamie. 'Can you smell that?'

Tom flapped his hand in front of his face. 'It's like rotten eggs,' he said. 'Worse than gingko.'

'What is it?' Jamie was holding his nose now.

GRUNK!

 Wanna stopped. He was trembling with fright, his eyes wild.

GRUNK, GRUNK!

'What's the matter, boy?' asked Jamie. 'Something's really bothering him.' Wanna dashed down the volcano and the boys hurried after him, worried.

Then the ground beneath them began to shake.

RUMMMMMMBLE!

'Feels like an earthquake,' cried Jamie, staggering on the shuddering rock. 'Wanna must have sensed it before we did.'

'Help!' The boys went sprawling on the stones. Wanna only kept his balance by spreading all four paws out wide.

The shaking stopped as suddenly as it had started.

Jamie jumped to his feet. 'Yow!' he exclaimed. 'The ground's really hot.'

'Hot ground, steamy rainwater, thick mist, strangely quiet plains.' Tom looked over at Jamie in horror. 'Uh oh.'

'This volcano isn't dormant at all,' said Jamie. 'It's active, and it's going to erupt!'

GARUMMBBLE!

The earth shook again, harder this time.

KABOOM!

The sound of a deafening explosion split the air and a massive cloud of black smoke blasted up from the volcano. Bright orange lava bubbled from the top. It poured over the side in a fast-flowing river.

'Look out!' cried Tom.

'It's heading straight for us!'

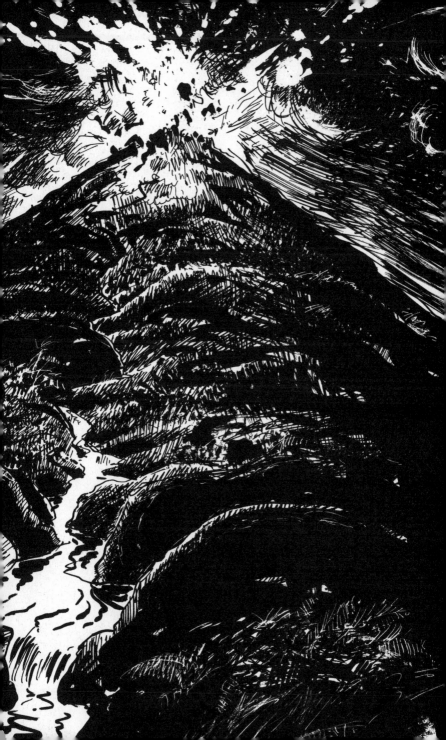

'Run!' shouted Jamie.

The lava flow was fast, very fast.
The boys turned and scrambled
down between the steep banks of the

stream bed. Wanna sent up a cloud of spray as he charged ahead.

Tom looked back over his shoulder. 'We've got to get out of this stream bed,' he yelled desperately. 'The lava's using it as a channel. And it's travelling much faster than we are.'

Jamie could see what he meant. The molten orange lava was taking the quickest route to get down the volcano—and they were right in its path.

Spitting and crackling, it surged towards them. Jamie started to haul himself up the slippery bank.

 255

GRUNK! GRUNK!

Jamie looked back. Wanna was trying in vain to climb out after them!

'Quick, Wanna!' yelled Jamie.

'We have to help him,' shouted Tom above the roar of the lava.

They flattened themselves on the bank, and Jamie could feel the heat of the approaching lava burning his arms. The boys grabbed a paw each and heaved Wanna to safety.

'Just in time!' said Tom, wiping the sweat from his forehead.

Wanna cowered behind them, watching the hot, spluttering flow

bubble past down the volcano.
Rocks popped with heat as
they were engulfed in the
boiling mass.

The boys
backed away,
shielding their
eyes from the
glare.

'I've never
felt anything so
hot,' said Jamie.

'We need to get to
the plains,' urged Tom.
'It's not safe here.'

They skidded down the

steep slope, jumping
over rocks and finally
pushing through ferns
near the bottom until they
ran out of breath.

Jamie took a quick glance
back and saw that the lava stream

hadn't reached as far as the green
lower slopes. 'Hey,' he panted. 'The
lava has stopped!'

Shielding his eyes, he followed
Jamie's gaze. 'It must have only been
a little eruption,' Tom guessed.

GRUNK!

Wanna started off again down the

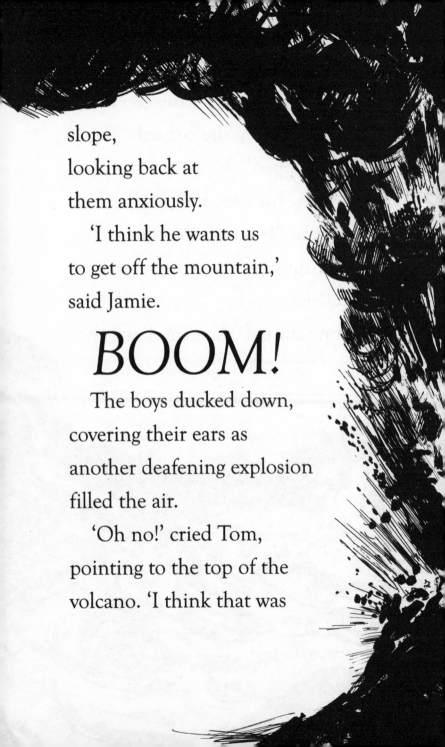

slope,
looking back at
them anxiously.

'I think he wants us
to get off the mountain,'
said Jamie.

BOOM!

The boys ducked down,
covering their ears as
another deafening explosion
filled the air.

'Oh no!' cried Tom,
pointing to the top of the
volcano. 'I think that was

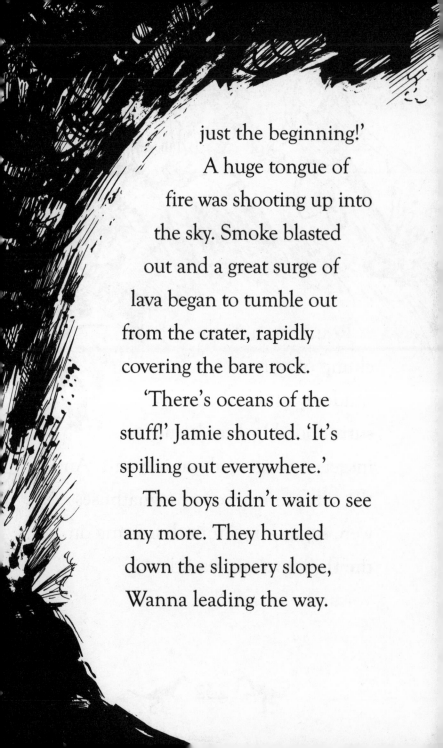

just the beginning!'
A huge tongue of
fire was shooting up into
the sky. Smoke blasted
out and a great surge of
lava began to tumble out
from the crater, rapidly
covering the bare rock.

'There's oceans of the
stuff!' Jamie shouted. 'It's
spilling out everywhere.'

The boys didn't wait to see
any more. They hurtled
down the slippery slope,
Wanna leading the way.

Rounding a dense
clump of ferns they
suddenly found themselves
surrounded by lizards and
insects swarming about in panic. And
the silly group of compsognathuses
were squawking around, feasting on
the fleeing creatures.

'I don't believe it!'
exclaimed Tom, trying
not to crush anything underfoot.

'They don't seem to realize the
volcano's spilling its guts,' Jamie said.
'They're just after snacks!'

Tom and Jamie looked at
each other. 'They're going to
get fried,' said Tom with
horror.

YAIEE! YAIEE! YAIEE! YAIEE!

YAIEE! YAIEE!

'We have to make them move,'
Jamie decided.

Tom waved his arms and ran at the
compsos. They ignored him and
carried on snacking, chirping happily
as they went.

'What are we going to do?' Jamie
looked round for an answer. The lava
had reached the top of the
vegetation. Bushes and ferns

YAIEE!

disappeared, burned to ashes as
they were engulfed by the rolling
wall of molten rock.

'Got an idea,' shouted Tom.

He ran among the
compsognathuses, letting out a loud,
YAIEE!

The little dinosaurs stopped and looked at him, open-mouthed. Tom squawked again. YAIEE!

The compsos copied him.

YAIEE! YAIEE!

'Now I've got their attention, show them some food,' Tom yelled.

Jamie pulled another sandwich out of the backpack. He waved it at the compsos. They smelled the ham and raced towards him, eyes shining greedily.

'Let's lure them away,' cried Tom.

Jamie held the sandwich above his head and the boys started to run down the mountain again. The band

of greedy compsos scampered after them.

'Got to go faster,' yelled Tom. 'The lava's getting closer.'

The boys pounded along as fast as they could. Jamie wondered how long he could keep up the pace. His heart was racing and his legs were hurting with every step. And he knew that the compsos couldn't run for as long as he could. The lava was rolling down in a sheet of searing orange heat—gaining on them with every second.

They were all going to be swallowed up.

With gasping breaths Jamie and
Tom crashed on through the ferns,
Wanna in the lead and the compsos
behind. Jamie could feel his heart
almost bursting from his chest as he

waited for the molten lava to surge over him.

But nothing happened. At last he couldn't bear it any longer. He threw a terrified glance over his shoulder. He expected to see a wall of bubbling lava about to crash down on him like a huge wave. But there was nothing there. Wiping the sweat from his eyes, he peered up the slope. High above, the lava was pouring into a new stream bed. It had found a quicker way down the mountain.

He bent double, trying to catch his breath. 'We can stop!' he yelled to Tom. 'The flow is heading away.

Towards Massive
Canyon.'

'What a relief!' Tom
punched the air.
'The canyon's deep
enough to take all
that lava.'

'That means
Jurassic Dino
World is safe, and
so are the
compsos,' added
Jamie as a bunch
of the little
creatures caught
up with them. Soon

the boys were surrounded by a sea of squawking dinosaurs, jumping for the sandwich that was still in Jamie's hand.

'Jump all you like!' Tom told them, laughing. 'We're just glad you didn't get covered in lava.'

Wanna ran around crossly head-butting the excited compsos away, but they ignored him and kept clamouring at the boys.

'This'll sort them out,' called Jamie. He broke the sandwich into small pieces, keeping it high above their heads. Then he threw the pieces in different directions.

All the compsognathuses' heads looked this way and that—and in an instant they scattered after the shower of food, squawking at the tops of their voices. The fastest ones swept the pieces up in their teeth and the

rest gave chase with their funny stiff-legged run.

'We've had an awesome adventure!' said Jamie, brushing volcanic dust out of his hair.

'Escape from the Jurassic volcano,'

announced Tom. 'It would make
a great TV programme.'

'Time to head home,' said Jamie,
turning towards Gingko Cave. 'To see
how Dad's got on with *his* greedy
dinosaurs.'

They stopped at the edge of the

jungle to take one last look at the
Misty Mountain with the thick
plume of smoke still rising from its
crater.

Tom breathed a sigh of relief. 'The
lava flow has stopped now.'

'There's a herd of brachiosaurs in

the distance,' said Jamie, pointing. 'And some diplodocuses nibbling at those trees over there.'

'The dinosaurs are all coming back to the plains,' said Tom.

'They must know the danger's over.'

'Everything is back to normal then,' said Jamie.

'Well,' said Tom, 'normal for our Jurassic World. And that's . . .'

'AWESOME!' they shouted together.

'Can't wait till next time,' said Jamie.

They plunged through the giant trees and splashed through a little river to get some of the volcanic dust off. Soon they had reached Gingko Cave.

Tom picked Wanna three juicy gingkoes from a nearby tree.

'Those greedy compsos shouldn't have all the fun, boy,' he said as he tossed them to their little dinosaur friend.

Wanna stuffed them all in his mouth at once and settled down to chomp. The boys waved goodbye, placed their feet into the dino footprints, and walked backwards into their own world.

As Jamie and Tom walked down the path to the beach, they heard shouts and cheers from below.

A crowd of dinosaurs was waving and beckoning at them. Dad and Grandad were standing in the middle, looking frazzled.

'Don't think we'll be able to escape this lot,' said Jamie as the boys headed along the beach.

Dad ran up. 'Thank goodness you're here!' he said. 'We're having a football match—carnivores versus herbivores. Will you referee?'

Grandad threw the ball to Jamie and the whistle to Tom. Jamie quickly placed the ball down on the sand for kick off and Tom blew the whistle to start the game.

In an instant every single footballer was charging towards them! Tom and Jamie were soon buried under a pile of cheering dinosaurs. At last a small pterodactyl got possession of the ball and all the others headed off after it, with a lot of prehistoric shrieking.

Jamie and Tom sat up and watched the eager herd make for the goal.

Tom grinned. 'I wonder who'd win if they played the compsognathuses!'

'I know one thing,' answered Jamie. 'I wouldn't want to be the referee for that match!'

DINOSAUR WORLD

- - - - BOYS' ROUTE

Massive Canyon

Humongous Waterfall

Plains

Fin Rock

Jurassic Ocean

Misty
Mountains

Thick Jungle

Gingko
Cave

Discovery
Hills

GLOSSARY

Allosaurus (al-oh-sor-us) – one of the largest meat-eating dinosaurs and one of the fiercest predators of its time. Its name means 'different lizard' because its backbone was shaped differently than other dinosaurs.

Ammonite (am-on-ite) – an extinct animal with octopus-like legs, and often a spiral-shaped shell, that lived in the ocean.

Apatosaurus (ap-at-oh-sor-us) – this plant-eating dinosaur was one of the biggest land animals with a large, long neck and tail but small head. Its name means 'deceptive lizard'. This dinosaur was formerly known as brontosaurus (see below).

Brontosaurus (bron-tow-sor-us) – scientists are now determined that brontosaurus fossils were not a new species but the same species known as apatosaurus (see above).

Ceratosaurus (se-rat-oh-sor-us) – meat-eating dinosaur that could run fast on its two back legs. Its front legs functioned more like hands with sharp claws. Its name means 'horned lizard' because of the short horn on the beast's nose.

Compsognathus (komp-sog-nay-thus) – a turkey-sized dinosaur that walked on two legs. The first dinosaur found with a reasonably complete skeleton, but not the smallest dinosaur as originally thought.

Gingko (gink-oh) – a tree native to China called a 'living fossil' because fossils of it have been found dating back millions of years, yet they are still around today. Also known as the stink bomb tree because of its smelly apricot-like fruit.

Jurassic (jur-as-sick) – from about 150 to 200 million years ago, the Jurassic Age was warm and humid, with lush jungle cover and great marine diversity. Large dinosaurs ruled on land, while the first birds took to the air.

Pangaea (pan-gee-ah) – a single continent that existed about 250 million years ago before the continents were separated into their current configuration.

Wannanosaurus (wah-nan-oh-sor-us) – a dinosaur that only ate plants and used its hard, flat skull to defend itself. Named after the place it was discovered: Wannano in China.